Path

Forward

by

NICOLE PYLAND

Path Forward

Celebrities Series Book #4

Jessica Morrison had made some mistakes in her life. Of all of them, one had caused her to lose the woman she had once thought she would spend the rest of her life with, along with the friends Jessica had thought of as family.

Venice Russo had somehow found herself in the company of a lot of beautiful, famous women. Dani Wilder, Peyton Gloss, Lennox Owen, Kenzie Smyth, and Maddox Delaney were now all her friends. That didn't stop Venice, who preferred to be called Val, from feeling a little out of place.

They nearly met at one fateful New Year's Eve party but happened to miss each other. A coincidence, or maybe fate, brings them together again. Jessica is carrying her baggage. Val doesn't feel like she has anything to look forward to in her life. When they find each other, they might also be able to find a path forward together.

To contact the author or for any additional information
visit: **https://nicolepyland.com**

BY THE AUTHOR

Stand-alone books:

- The Fire
- The Moments
- The Disappeared
- Reality Check

Chicago Series:

- Introduction – Fresh Start
- Book #1 – The Best Lines
- Book #2 – Just Tell Her
- Book #3 – Love Walked into The Lantern
- Series Finale – What Happened After

San Francisco Series:

- Book #1 – Checking the Right Box
- Book #2 – Macon's Heart
- Book #3 – This Above All
- Series Finale – What Happened After

Tahoe Series:

- Book #1 – Keep Tahoe Blue

- Book #2 – Time of Day
- Book #3 – The Perfect View
- Book #4 – Begin Again
- Series Finale – What Happened After

Celebrities Series:

- Book #1 – No After You
- Book #2 – All the Love Songs
- Book #3 – Midnight Tradition
- Book #4 – The Path Forward
- Series Finale – What Happened After

Sports Series:

- Book #1 – Always More
- Book #2 – A Shot at Gold
- Book #3 – The Unexpected Dream
- Book #4 – Finding a Keeper

CONTENTS

CHAPTER 1

"JESSICA!"

"Over here!"

"Jessica, look!"

She was used to the shouting. She had heard it nearly daily from the age of fifteen when she had been in her first runway show. One day, she had been a normal thirteen-year-old girl, walking dog on the sidewalk in front of her house. The next minute, a model scout that had, apparently, been visiting her mother across the street, noticed her and asked if she could talk to Jessica's parents. They had signed a contract with a major agency on her behalf a few months later. She had started in print, as most young models do. Then, she had landed a few local commercials followed by two national ones. Finally, Jessica had been asked to walk a runway in a real show in New York Fashion Week.

Today, though, was Jessica's thirty-fifth birthday, and her life had changed a lot in the past twenty years. In some ways, her life was better. She was now a model-turned-movie-star, with enough money to last her a lifetime. In other ways, she wondered if it was worse. She had many acquaintances, but she wasn't convinced any of them were really her friends. She also had no girlfriend to speak of, after making some pretty terrible decisions in her previous long-term relationship. Sure, she had gone on dates since they had ended; she had also had sex since. But she hadn't found anyone who had ever just fit. She knew the breakup was her fault. Jessica thought about it and regretted her actions every day, but it wouldn't change the past.

"I was thinking we could skip out on the rest of this thing once you're off the carpet," Lisa Grandy told her.

"I'm not skipping the premiere of my first movie as a lead, Lisa," she whispered over at her.

"I'm on a plane tomorrow at six in the morning, Jessica. If we stay for this whole thing, that doesn't give us much time to–"

"Hook up?" Jessica asked, smiling in the direction of the cameras and then looking over at Lisa. "I didn't invite you to this thing, Lisa. You took the job as a costume designer after I was already on board. I told you this was a bad idea."

"Let's just…" Lisa nodded to the side and moved away from the cameras and microphones behind a partition likely set up just for this very purpose; two people having a semi-private conversation. "Jess, just tell me what you want. This whole back-and-forth thing is getting old, and I'm not getting any younger."

"Aren't you tired of all this?" Jessica asked softly, leaning down a little toward the shorter woman.

"I've told you more than once that it doesn't just have to be sex with us. We were together before, and–"

"No, we weren't," Jessica told her and sighed. "We weren't. I was with Maddox, and I was cheating on Maddox with you."

"But, we were together." Lisa moved to take her hand, but Jessica pulled it away. "I know you were with her, but it was long-distance. You and I weren't long-distance. For months, it was just the two of us; and it worked, Jess. I've been your fuck buddy ever since you two ended for good, and I'm turning forty this year. I shouldn't even be using the phrase 'fuck buddy.'" The woman chuckled a little and asked, "So, tonight, we can go back to your place or mine, and we can talk about what this could be and make love, and I can catch my flight tomorrow morning knowing that

I have a girlfriend back in LA; or we can call this what it is and just end it."

Jessica looked behind her, where her assistant, Carol, was glaring at her that she needed to get inside. A Carol-glare was not to be ignored, regardless of what Jessica was doing when she received it. Jessica turned back to Lisa and thought about the fact that she had made yet another mistake. That was her new normal. She would make one, attempt to fix it, make another, and it would continue. At some point, she'd have to stop making so many mistakes and finally do something right in her life.

"After that night, where we ran into Maddox at the New Year's party, I shouldn't have gone home with you, Lisa." She swallowed and said, "It's not fair to you."

"So, this is over?" Lisa asked.

"You deserve better than me." Jessica laughed softly. "Trust me; you're an amazing designer, you're smart, talented, beautiful, sexy, and you're crazy good in the bedroom." She laughed a little more, trying to break the tension.

"But you don't want anything more from me than sex?" Lisa asked, crossing her arms over her chest now.

"Friendship," Jessica replied.

"That's called a fuck buddy, Jess."

"No, I mean, I just want friendship."

"So, no more sex? We're just going to be friends after years of being on and off, and then on again?"

"If you want more than friends with benefits, I don't think I'm your girl, Lisa."

"You don't seem too thrilled about those benefits these days, anyway," Lisa replied.

"I think I want the same thing you do."

"I want you," Lisa said, again reaching for Jessica's hand, but being denied. "I always have. I know we started off on the wrong foot because you were with someone else, but I think we've stayed in each other's lives for a reason, Jess. I've always wanted more than what you've given me."

"Jess, we have to get inside," Carol said, interrupting them obviously reluctantly. "I'm sorry. You still have a few spots to hit for the cameras, and then we need to get in there."

"It's fine," Lisa said, waving Carol off. "I'm done. We're done."

"Lisa, we can talk more about it later. I just–"

"No, it's fine. You're right. We're both looking for the same thing. It's just not something we can have together."

"I'm sorry," Jessica replied.

"So am I." Lisa swiped down the front of her black dress pants and put on a brave smile. "Game faces, ladies."

They walked back out to the carpet, where Lisa left quickly to get inside the theater. Jessica stood on her mark, smiled as if nothing had happened, and then went inside as well. As she watched the premiere of the film she had worked so hard on, she could only think of all the mistakes she had made in getting here.

She had cheated on Maddox, the woman she had once thought she would marry. She had done that twice, technically. She had slept with Lisa for months before the affair came out and Maddox dumped her. When Maddox had agreed to give her another chance, Jessica ruined that, too. She had kissed another woman. It hadn't gone any further than that, but she had hated herself that night. Jessica had hated herself even more when Maddox dumped her for the final time. She had put her girlfriend through hell. And now, here she was: still single on her thirty-fifth birthday, disappointing a woman who actually wanted to be with her because Jessica was restless and needed something new. She needed someone new.

The following morning, after spending the rest of her night out at a party in her honor, Jessica awoke slightly hungover and not at all ready to start her day. She grunted a few times, because she should not have had that much to drink, and rolled over onto her back. She checked the bed then, and it was empty. That was good. She had only done it a handful of times, and mostly after runway shows in her twenties, but she had sometimes woken in her bed to a woman next to her with no clothes and no name that she could remember.

She stood up and stretched, knowing a cold shower would help set her right. She removed her shorts, panties, and the tank top she had thrown on before climbing into bed the previous night. The cold shower was only step one to her recovery. Step two was a smoothie made by Carol, which knowing her amazing assistant, was likely already prepared and sitting on her kitchen counter.

She dressed in a new shorts/shirt combo and walked slowly and carefully down the stairs. She turned the corner and entered her kitchen but saw no smoothie. There was also no Carol. Jessica went to the sliding glass door that led outside to her small backyard with only enough space for a pool and a hot tub because then came the cliffs and the remarkable view of Los Angeles beyond. She remembered that Carol sometimes went for a morning swim before taking a shower in the guest bathroom. Jessica had never had a problem with her assistant using anything she needed at her place, but then it dawned on her.

"She's not here," Jessica said to herself, turning back around as she remembered.

Carol was on vacation for a week. It was the first vacation the woman had taken in over two years, despite Jessica telling her she could take care of herself for at least two weeks a year. Carol was dedicated to her job, though; and also probably to the healthy salary she paid her.

Well, this meant Jessica would have to make her own smoothie. This was not a problem. She could do it. First, she'd have to find the blender. She stared at her kitchen cabinets as if one of them would magically open on its own and reveal the appliance. When it didn't, she gave in and opened each door until she found it in the bottom cabinet behind a few pots and pans. Jessica pulled it out, growling as she did, because the headache was getting worse, and bending over and fussing with pans really wasn't helping. She would talk to Carol about reorganizing the cabinets or, better yet, she could do it herself one day.

Jessica plugged it in where she had seen Carol use it before and opened her two-door clear glass fridge to stare at it without pulling anything out. She had no idea what went into this smoothie Carol made for her at least a couple of times a month. She knew what she could taste. There was banana definitely and some blueberries. She also thought there was at least kale in it, and maybe spinach. Other than that, she'd be guessing. So, she pulled out the giant tub of Greek yogurt, one banana, the bag of fresh spinach, some kale, and a small container of blueberries. She dumped it all into the blender, hoping for the best, put the lid on tight because she was not about to clean up a mess this morning, and started the device. She then let the blades spin and spin, closing her eyes at the noxious sound. When her drink was made, she poured it unceremoniously into a large glass, left the remnants in the blender, and took a drink.

"Shit! That's disgusting," she blurted out, wiping her mouth. "I can't even make a fucking smoothie right."

Jessica left the still full glass in the sink and walked into the living room, where she flopped down onto the sofa her interior designer had picked out for her. She had nothing to do today. She would have a few more press junkets for the movie and some morning shows over the next couple of weeks, but today, she had nothing to do. She was thirty-five now; not exactly at the top of the call sheet for magazine covers, photo shoots, or runways anymore. She had successfully managed to move into acting, unlike so many others, but even if she shot two movies a year, she'd still have at least a couple of months off with nothing to do with them.

Her phone beeped from its place on the table. She must have left it there before she'd gone to bed last night. She grabbed it and checked the notification. It was an email from the delivery company that was supposed to deliver a new pair of shoes to her place. Unfortunately, it said they hadn't been able to make the delivery due to her security gate and would be leaving those shoes at one of their ship centers, or she could fill out a form and have them redeliver the package tomorrow. Jessica had nothing to do for work today, but she had planned on going out tonight. There was a new lesbian bar in town, which was a miracle since most lesbian bars in the country had started to disappear years ago. She had planned to make a brief appearance to see if it was a place she would like to hang out at in the future. If she met a beautiful woman who wanted to go on a real date with her and not just have a night of hot sex, that would be even better. If not, at least she was putting herself back out there.

Since it was just going to be a quick visit, Jessica had planned to wear her new shoes: gladiator-style sandals by one of her favorite designers. For a second, she thought about just wearing another pair, but then she looked around the spotless living room and wondered what she would do today if she didn't go to this place in North Hollywood and pick up her shoes. She made herself some coffee, forgetting about the smoothie, drank it down as she pulled her hair back, put on a pair of dark sunglasses and a hat with the Dodgers' logo on it to help her blend in, and got into her silver Tesla Model X. Then, she set off for her new shoes, and likely, a lunch in an outdoor, trendy place where she could be seen but not really be seen.

CHAPTER 2

"WE'LL have that sent today for you," Val said.

"Thanks. And, my tracking number?" the man asked.

"It's right there on your receipt," she said, pointing at the receipt she had just handed him.

"Right. Thanks." The man turned and walked toward the door.

Val had managed this pack and ship store for the past two years, starting as a regular hourly employee two years prior to that and then getting promoted. It was a job that had turned into an unexpected career. Val hadn't been the girl who grew up knowing exactly what she wanted to do. She had been the girl who envied those girls. They had wanted to be doctors, lawyers, teachers, writers, singers, and just about everything else. Val had listened to all of them talk about their futures and wondered about her own. She thought about those girls as she lifted the small box from the scale and moved it behind the counter, placing it on the top of the pile.

Had they all followed their dreams? Were they now doctors and lawyers, or had they done something else with their lives? Val was almost thirty-six now. She had a career that she enjoyed enough to keep doing without going after anything else. She had a couple of close friends that were more like family, and she had a nice apartment that she shared with one of them. She did not have the other things she had always known she wanted. From an early age, she had known she wanted to be married and have kids. As she looked at the wall calendar with the cute picture of a kitten on the wall, she thought that wasn't very likely anymore.

"Excuse me," a voice said just as Val turned around.

"Oh, sorry. What can I do for you?" she asked, giving the woman her customer-service smile.

"I had a package dropped off here when they couldn't deliver it to my house," the tall woman said.

"Do you have a tracking number?" Val asked, logging into the computer in front of her.

"Yeah, hold on." The woman pulled out her phone and scrolled until she turned it to face Val.

"May I?" Val asked, nodding toward it.

"Sure," the woman said, handing her the device.

Val's fingers brushed the woman's as she took the phone from her, and Val caught herself looking at this woman more closely. She was wearing dark glasses, so Val couldn't see her eyes, but her skin looked flawless; her lips were full, and she was tall. Val had gotten used to celebrities living in Los Angeles. She guessed this was one of them but couldn't tell which one with the glasses and hat getting in her way. She focused on the phone then, not wanting to be obvious with her staring, typed the number into her system, and passed the phone back to her.

"We don't have it here yet," she said.

"What do you mean?"

"It was supposed to be delivered this morning," Val replied.

"Right. I know that," the woman said, tucking her phone back into her designer bag.

"It takes a day for them to get it to us," Val told her. "It's probably still in the truck. They'll bring it here at the end of their route. Then, we can mark it here in our system, and you'll be notified that you can come get it."

The woman slid off her sunglasses and looked down at Val's chest.

"Venice?" she questioned like so many other people did. "Pretty name," she said in a near-whisper.

"They make us put our real names on the nametags, but I go by Val," she replied.

"And there's really nothing you can do?" the woman asked, setting the sunglasses on the bill of the hat.

"I'm afraid not. It should be here tomorrow, or you can have it delivered to another location. There should be a form in the email you received."

"I guess I'll just have to wear another pair of shoes tonight," the woman said.

Now that Val could see her eyes, she was taken aback by their hazel color, and it took her a minute to respond.

"A gift for yourself?" she asked, making conversation since there were no other customers, and her only employee working today was at lunch.

"You could say that." The woman smiled at her. "It really is a pretty name," she added, sliding the sunglasses back on, turning, and leaving the shop.

"Hey, I'm back," Nick, her only employee, said as he passed the exiting woman on his way back into the shop. "Give me, like, five, and I'll clock back in, so you can grab something to eat. I just have to pee, and the bathroom at the Subway on the corner is employee's only."

"Sure. Okay," Val replied, not really listening.

Nick walked into the back room of the shop and, likely, into the bathroom. Val stood there semi-frozen for a long minute before the next customer came in. She took care of him, helping him make a quick copy on their self-serve copy machine. When Nick came back out wearing his uniform blue vest and nametag, Val knew he was back on the clock.

"You got this?" she asked, referring to the man who would need to pay.

"I got it," Nick replied, smiling at the man. "Just one copy, sir?"

Val didn't hear the response. She went into the back room and opened the small refrigerator to retrieve the lunch she'd brought. She usually just ate back here and scrolled through nothing of consequence on her phone. She pulled the turkey sandwich out of the clear plastic bag and set it back down on top of it, staring at it as if it would suddenly turn into something she actually wanted to eat.

"Screw it," she said as she stood.

She lived in Los Angeles, in North Hollywood – there were restaurants all over the place. She could go out for lunch for once, actually enjoy what she ate, and return to work not pondering what TV dinner she'd throw in the microwave tonight.

"Hey, I'll be back in an hour. If it picks up, though, just call my cell. I'll come right back," she told Nick.

"No problem," he replied and went back to replacing the paper in the copier.

Val pulled her sunglasses on as she hit the sidewalk on the busy street, and looked up and down, trying to figure out where to go. She had been to many of these places before; not usually for lunch, but she knew what they offered. There was the tapas place on the left, but they didn't open until four. There was the Italian place on the right, but she wasn't in the mood for anything heavy, and all Italian food was heavy. She should know; she was Italian. It was the American bistro down the street for the win. She had only been there once, and she had liked the Caesar salad. That was light enough and filling since she would add chicken to it. Val walked down the street until she arrived at the two rows of outdoor tables. That was when she saw her.

"Shit," Val muttered under her breath. "She's going to think I'm stalking her or something."

The woman with the hat and sunglasses had just received her iced tea and was looking down at her phone. Val was pretty sure she hadn't been seen yet. She could turn around and go for Italian after all. Too late. The woman looked up from her phone, noticed her, and then looked around the tables, likely expecting Val to be joining someone for lunch. They were only about ten feet apart. The restaurant wasn't crowded, at least not outside.

"Sorry, I'm not like following you or anything," Val said.

"I didn't think you were," the woman replied.

"I was just going to grab something for lunch. I'll hit the carry-out counter," she said, pointing to the door.

"You're allowed to eat at a table like everyone else, Venice," the woman said.

"Val," she replied.

"Your nametag said Venice." The woman smirked at her.

"That is my given name, yes." Val pressed her hands against the railing separating the restaurant tables from the sidewalk. "But I go by Val."

"Well, I like Venice better than Val. I knew a Val once. She was a bitch," she said.

"Okay. I'll just grab my salad and leave you to your lunch."

"How long do you have?"

"I'm sorry?" Val said.

"For lunch? How long do you have?"

"An hour."

"Plenty of time. Join me." The woman motioned to the empty table. "I'm eating alone."

"I can't get the package to you any sooner if we eat lunch together," Val joked.

"I wasn't trying to bribe you for shoes, Venice. I have hundreds of shoes. I have no shortage of shoes to choose from tonight." The woman laughed a little. "If you're eating here, you can join me. If not, that's okay, too."

Val swallowed. Then, she hopped the railing and moved between two empty tables to get to the woman's table. That was when it dawned on her.

"I don't even know your name," Val said as she sat down.

"Jessica," she replied.

"Nice to meet you, Jessica." Val held out her hand for her to shake.

"We're getting formal now, huh?" Jessica smiled but shook Val's hand. "And, be honest. Do you hate the name

Venice and want me to call you Val, or is it just that everyone asks you how you got the name and you're annoyed with answering?"

"The latter more than the former," Val replied.

"Then, I'll call you Venice." She nodded.

"Okay," Val said, laughing.

"Can I get you something to drink?" the waitress asked her.

"Just water," Val replied. "Can I actually order a chicken Caesar salad to go as well?"

"Of course. I'll put that in for you." The waitress walked off.

"I thought you were staying," Jessica said.

"I shouldn't interrupt your lunch like this. I can eat back at the store."

Jessica took a drink and said, "If that's what you want."

"I'm sorry. She just walked away. Did I hijack your lunch order?"

"No, I ordered before you got here," Jessica replied.

Then, they just sat there looking in every direction except at each other for a long minute.

"I should just go. This is weird."

"Why?"

"You don't know me. You're a customer. I should just wait inside for my food."

"How long have you worked there?" Jessica asked.

The waitress returned with Val's water, placed it in front of her, and disappeared again.

"Four years," Val said without thinking.

"Do you like it?"

"It's fine," she answered.

"Fine, but not great?"

"I like it enough to buy my own franchise," Val said, taking a drink of her water.

"You own that place?" Jessica asked.

"No, but I'm saving to buy one."

"Oh, cool." She nodded.

"What do you do?" Val asked.

"I'm a model and actress. I guess I'm more actress than model these days," Jessica replied.

Then, Val put it together.

"Jessica Morrison," she said. "I should have realized it sooner. We just shipped about a hundred posters for your new movie. We get a lot of studio stuff."

"That's me," she replied as the waitress placed a salad in front of Jessica and then a different one inside a plastic container in front of Val.

"Did you need the shoes for a premiere or something?"

Jessica seemed a little confused for a moment and said, "No, they were just for tonight. I'm going to a new lesbian bar tonight. I was going to wear them."

"Got it," Val replied, grabbing her container. "Can I have the check?" she asked the waitress before she could walk off again.

"I'll take care of it," Jessica said. "Just put it on mine," she told the waitress.

"No, I can't let you do that," Val replied, pulling her wallet out of her back pocket.

"Yes, you can. It's a Caesar salad. I think I can take care of it for you." Jessica laughed a little.

"Well, I did add chicken," Val replied as she stood.

"In that case, you can eat it here with me. Then, I'll pay. I think that's a fair exchange."

Val had two options. She could sit and eat this salad with Jessica Morrison, the woman she'd seen on a billboard when she had driven to work, and then let her pay for it, or she could just drop a twenty on the table and thank her for the offer.

"If I sit and eat with you, I'll pay for it myself. Deal?" Val chose option three.

"You drive a hard bargain, Venice." Jessica pulled the sunglasses off her eyes, winked at Val, and placed them on the table. "Deal."

"Well, okay."

"She's eating here. Can she get a plate?" Jessica asked the waitress.

"No, it's okay." Val waved her off. "I'll just eat it in this."

"Like a barbarian?" Jessica teased.

"Well, I'm definitely not as civilized as Jessica Morrison." Val smiled over at her. "I'm okay," she said to the waitress, who was still standing there.

"Let me know if there's anything else you need," she said and walked inside.

"So, Venice. Where did it come from?"

"I should have made another deal with you. If you call me Venice, you can't ask me where it comes from?"

"Did your parents conceive you there, so you just always think of them getting busy in a gondola or something?" Jessica asked, taking a bite.

"God!" Val laughed. "No. They just got married there and liked it. That's it. That's the story. They spent a crap ton of money they didn't really have on a celebration across the globe and then had their honeymoon there. That's all."

"Then, why do you hate it so much?"

"I don't hate it. I just get asked the question about ten times a day at work, so I–"

"Right. Sorry," Jessica interrupted and looked down at her plate.

"No, I didn't mean you. I mean, yeah, you did ask me, and technically you are a customer, but I didn't mean you."

"Why do I get the special exemption?" the woman asked, looking up at her.

"You're the millionth customer, I guess," Val replied with a smile.

They finished their salads, talking about nothing in particular. When the check came, Jessica tried once more to pay for the whole thing, but Val reminded her of their deal and paid for her own salad.

"I have to get back," she told Jessica.

"I should get going, too." Jessica stood.

Val stood and asked, "Do you have an interview or a photo shoot or something?"

"No plans today; just the bar for an hour or so tonight."

"Making an appearance?" she asked.

"No. I just want to check it out, see if I like it, and if I do, maybe I'll go back sometime." Jessica picked up her purse.

"Well, I'm sorry you have to find other shoes to wear, but I hope you have a good time."

"Thanks." Jessica moved her top lip to one side and her bottom to the other side and added, "You should come."

"Where? To the bar?"

"Yeah, it's around here. I don't know. Maybe it's not your scene?"

Val knew what she was asking.

"I'm not much for bars," she replied with a smirk.

"But you are for lesbians?" Jessica asked with a lifted eyebrow.

"Some of them, yes," Val replied.

Jessica smiled a little wider and said, "It's called Wonderland because, of course, it is."

"I've heard of it." Val nodded.

"Maybe I'll see you there tonight," Jessica replied.

Val nodded again, smiled, and said, "It was nice meeting you."

CHAPTER 3

JESSICA should have told Venice what time she was going to be here. She had been sitting here for over an hour, watching the door, waiting for the woman to arrive, and turning down potential dates left and right.

"Can I buy you a drink?" a woman wearing not one but two flannel shirts asked her.

"I'm okay, but thank you," she replied, lifting her completely full glass as evidence.

The woman nodded at her and walked off, rocking that red and black flannel shirt wrapped around her waist and the one she had on over a white tank top. She wasn't exactly Jessica's type, but Jessica wasn't sure what her type was anymore. The only woman she had ever actually been in love with had been Maddox, and she wasn't butch or particularly femme. There were times Jessica wanted her to be more in both of those directions, but it didn't matter anymore. They were done, and Maddox had a girlfriend that, from what Jessica had heard, she had just bought a house with.

When the bar door opened, three women entered. Venice was not among them. Jessica waited another twenty minutes, turned down one woman for a dance, another one for a drink, a third for a conversation, and finished her drink. Then, she left, ordering a car on her way out since she had been smart enough not to drive to the bar. When she climbed into bed later, she couldn't get rid of the feeling of disappointment. Her lunch with Venice had been the only highlight of her day; her entire week, really. Lisa had texted her that afternoon that she'd have someone send whatever stuff Jessica had left at her place. Jessica couldn't think of anything she had left at Lisa's. They usually had sex, and then whoever didn't live wherever they were, would leave. Sometimes, they just hung out and talked, but it wasn't like Jessica brought anything or left it there.

The following morning, she went for a run on her treadmill, took a shower, and looked up a recipe for a smoothie she could make with what she had in her fridge. She drank it down, and it wasn't terrible. Then, she waited for the call from the radio station. She would do a phone interview today for a morning show, and then she had a taping of a late-night show in the afternoon. She had a few hours in between, and her evening was free, so it wasn't a crazy busy day. Jessica was used to crazy busy days, though, and she kind of missed them if she was being honest. She had no idea what to do with herself on her days off now, so she got dressed and decided to go out to lunch. Then, she remembered that she never filled out the stupid form for the package. She smiled and thanked past Jessica for giving her an excuse to see the woman that had captured her attention yesterday.

"I'm looking for a package," Jessica said and couldn't stop herself from smiling.

"Jessica?" Venice asked.

"I'm glad you didn't forget all about me," she replied.

Venice gave her a look that told Jessica that she was crazy, and said, "I didn't think you'd come in. I assumed you'd have it delivered to your place." Venice walked up to the computer. "Can I have the tracking number again?"

"All business, huh?" Jessica asked but passed her the phone all the same.

"You're here for the shoes, right?" she asked, typing something.

"And for some answers." Jessica leaned on the counter. "I seem to recall inviting you out last night."

"You did?" Venice asked.

"Wonderland? Ring any bells?"

"You said you were going, and that I could check it out if I wanted."

"Yeah, that's an invite," Jessica replied.

"Oh, I just thought… I don't know. I guess I just thought you said that to be polite or something. That was an invite?"

"That may be the first time I've ever been accused of being polite," Jessica replied, still smiling at her. "I went. Did you show, and I missed you?"

"No, I stayed in," Venice replied, walking away for a second to grab the package. She returned with it, scanned it, and passed it to her. "Here you go."

"Thanks," Jessica said, taking it from her. "Did I put you off or something yesterday?"

"What? Why?"

"I don't know. I thought we got along, and I invited you out. Then, you didn't show up."

"I guess we got our wires crossed," Venice replied.

"Right," Jessica said, lowering her head to the package to make sure it was hers. "Well, I should get going. I have an interview in an hour."

Two customers walked through the door. Jessica turned around and hoped they'd be here to buy some office supplies or make a copy, but no such luck. Both of them entered the line right behind her.

"I'll be with you in one second," Venice said to them.

"I'll let you go," Jessica told her, standing up to her full height. "Thanks for the shoes."

"Jessica, I'm–"

"Have a good day, Venice," she interrupted.

Had she been that unclear yesterday when she had asked Venice to meet her at the bar? She must have been. She replayed the conversation in her mind, trying to find where she had messed up. She hadn't exactly been direct, and she also wasn't one hundred percent sure Venice was gay. She did have an idea that Venice was at least into women, all labels aside. Her hair was on the shorter side and was a deep, rich brown. Her eyes matched the color, and her skin looked light caramel and smooth. The woman wasn't as tall as Jessica, but she was used to that. Jessica was 5'10" and, technically, on the shorter side of many of her model friends, but she had always been taller than the women she dated. Venice hadn't asked her any questions about her job. She hadn't been curious about her celebrity friends, or what it was like to work on a movie. She hadn't asked her anything, really. Normally, Jessica spent conversations with non-industry people talking only about the industry, when she just wanted to get to know whoever she was talking to and have them get to know her in return.

After Jessica's interview, she returned home and planned to spend a quiet night in maybe doing some online shopping. She didn't need anything, but she had been wanting to look at the new spring collections. She missed that part of the job. She was no longer the model they called to wear stuff in print ads or walk them on the runway, so she didn't have the insider scoop she was used to. Instead, she perused the same sites that others did to find out what was the new trend of the season. Apparently, the eighties were coming back this year. Jessica snacked on some rice cakes, which used to be part of her daily diet, but now, she just ate because she actually liked them. She scrolled on her smart TV through several fashion sites and blogs to see the bright neon oranges, yellows, and greens.

Yeah, she was bored. She was a bored little rich girl. Jessica sighed. She no longer fit the girl part of that cliché. She was a bored, fully grown woman with nothing to do but wallow in her loneliness. When her phone rang, she thought for a second that it might be someone calling to invite her out for the night, but then she saw Carol's name.

"Hey, you're supposed to be on vacation," she said when she picked up.

"I am on vacation. I am sitting on a beach with an umbrella drink next to me, so I'm fine. How are you? Do you want me to put in a grocery order for you or something?"

"Carol, I can order my own groceries," she said, laughing at her assistant's thoughtfulness. "You're off the clock. Just enjoy your trip."

"Okay. Well, I just got an email from that gallery you like. They have an event tonight if you're interested. I forwarded you the invite."

"For tonight?"

"Yeah, I swear I didn't miss an email from them. Maybe they're just late getting the invites out, or my email crapped out on me or something. Anyway, I sent it to you. If you need me to order a car for you or–"

"I probably won't even go. But if I do, I will order my own car. You have fun on the beach with your boyfriend, and don't do any work until you get back, okay?"

"Fine. Fine. I'm a workaholic, I know. Someone has to keep you in line, though," Carol joked.

"You can keep me in line when you get back. I've managed to make all my appointments and feed myself in the past two days."

"Okay. I'll trust you. By the way, if you go, and you end up drinking too much, the hangover smoothie recipe is in your junk drawer."

"Wait. It is?"

"Yeah, I wrote it down. Just make sure you don't drink too much so you won't need it, okay?"

"I'll be good, Mom," she teased. "Have an amazing time, okay?"

"I will. Bye, Jess."

"Bye."

Jessica hung up and opened her email app to see that the show tonight at her favorite art gallery was for none other than Dani Wilder. She thought about texting Carol back that the woman should have known Jessica wouldn't want to go to this show, but she didn't want to interrupt the vacation she had just told her to get back to. God, Dani

Wilder. Jessica hadn't seen her since that New Year's Eve party when she'd run into Maddox, almost fucked Lisa in the guest bedroom just because she had needed to feel something, and then did actually fuck her back at her place. It had been a mistake going to that party, but she'd gone because she just wanted some closure.

That had been pretty stupid, too. Maddox hadn't been ready for her apology the first thousand times Jessica had made it. She still wasn't ready for it at the party last year. Jessica shouldn't have tried to force it. If they were ever going to have another conversation about what happened between them, it would have to be on Maddox's terms. Jessica knew that it was likely Maddox would be there tonight. Maddox, Dani, Peyton, and Maddox's girlfriend, Avery, were all good friends. She used to be able to count herself amongst that group, along with Lennox, who was now married to Kenzie. She hadn't spent much time with Kenzie, but she had with Lennox, Peyton, and Dani. She hated that she'd not only lost her girlfriend because of her actions but also all the friends she'd gained through their relationship.

Dani had been the one she'd technically known the longest. They had both been models. They had run in similar circles and had even shared a couple of covers. She had always liked Dani's kindness, openness, and that she tried to understand people. Dani had pretty much retired from modeling and had taken up photography even more so in recent years. She had also gotten married to Peyton and had become a mother two times over. Jessica hadn't talked to her, but she'd read an article or two where Dani said she was done modeling and wanted to focus on her family and her photography now.

Jessica wouldn't mind seeing Dani. She'd like the opportunity to apologize for what she did at the party, at the very least, and maybe even buy one of Dani's pieces, which she knew would be good. Maddox had helped teach the woman, after all, and Maddox was incredibly talented.

Jessica still had a black and white photo on her bedroom wall of a deer in the woods that Maddox had taken. She just couldn't take it down. It was that good.

She knew that if Dani was there, Peyton would be there. If Lennox or Kenzie were in town, they'd be there, too. She shouldn't go. That was how bad breakups worked: the one that made the mistake loses the shared friends. But she could at least just say she was sorry for her behavior at the party and leave if they weren't interested in hearing about it. She did need to check one thing, though. She opened her social media apps on her phone, one after the other, stalked her ex-girlfriend, and determined that, according to Facebook and Twitter, Maddox was on a job in Seattle. That made her decision a little bit easier.

Jessica read the details of the invite again, discovered it was a black-tie affair, and went in search of something to wear. She took another shower, pulled her hair back into an intricate bun, put on her makeup, choosing a smoky-eye to go with her black cocktail dress, and slid those gladiator sandals she just received onto her feet. It wasn't the most formal look, but it was formal enough for an opening.

She decided as she ordered a car for herself that she would be brave tonight. She would start to put the past version of herself, the one that had messed everything up, behind her; and hopefully, the women she'd encounter tonight would be okay with her trying to do just that.

CHAPTER 4

VAL had only agreed to come tonight because her friends had insisted she needed to get out of her apartment. It was true; she'd been spending a lot of time alone lately. There wasn't a reason for her self-imposed seclusion. She hadn't gone through a recent breakup or a work setback. Her family was fine; no one had gotten sick or died. She just wasn't interested in going out in Los Angeles anymore. She had been going out in Los Angeles since before she turned twenty-one. Now, she was in her mid-thirties, still single, and not likely to find the girl of her dreams at some lesbian nightspot or in a café.

She had promised, though, and tonight wasn't about dating or even making friends. It was about celebrating a woman Val couldn't believe would call her a friend to begin with. It had all happened a couple of years ago. A woman she had been dating at the time had been interested in photography and suggested they take a class together as a joint hobby and a way to spend more time together. Val had gone along with the plan. Little did she know, Dani Wilder would be in that class as well. The relationship hadn't lasted, but she had gotten to know Dani a little throughout the course. Dani had then invited Val to her New Year's Eve party at the house she shared with her wife, Peyton Gloss.

That had been the true beginning of their friendship and Val's friendship with Maddox Delaney and Avery

Simpson. The couple had met that night and had been together ever since. Val just felt lucky Maddox hadn't tried to kill her that night, since Val had been interested in Avery, too. She didn't hang out with them often. Peyton was usually either touring or recording, and Dani was typically with her if the woman was on tour, bringing their kids along with them. Maddox was in town most of the time these days since she was taking a break from international travel, but she did still take jobs and travel within the States.

Maddox had been the one to convince her to go. Dani had sent the invite, but Maddox had told her to attend. She had even made a comment that Peyton had convinced her to go to that New Year's Eve party when she had been reluctant, and she ended up meeting the love of her life that night. Val wasn't sure if Maddox expected her to meet the love of her life tonight, but she had rented a tux, which, surprisingly, wasn't all that difficult in this town. She had thought finding one that was cut for a woman would be a problem, and she would have to just wear a jacket and tie, but she managed to find a place that rented by the day or week that had a woman's tux that fit her fairly well.

She straightened the tie before she climbed out of the Lyft she had ordered because she didn't want to have to worry about finding parking, and straightened her jacket when she got out. She had only worn a tux one other time in her life. That had been for a wedding between one of her childhood friends and her now wife. She felt pretty lucky growing up in LA. She'd known of four other lesbians in her local high school, and three of them had been out when they had been there. She hadn't felt bullied much, just a few comments here and there from some boys commenting that they'd like to watch, but that was all bravado and hormones. Val made it through okay and was still grateful that that was all she'd had to deal with.

"Invitation, please," the man, also dressed in a tuxedo, standing at the door, said.

"Here you go," Val replied, showing him her phone.

The guy nodded and said, "Welcome." Then, he opened the clear glass door for her and motioned for her to go in.

Security must be tight given who the show was for and the fact that she was married to Peyton Gloss. Val knew Peyton and Dani had to practically surround themselves with security whenever they went out in public. Tonight would be no exception. Val walked through the door and into the wide-open gallery with plain white walls specifically kept that way in order to let the audience focus on the photographs hanging on them. The lighting that was not focused on the photography was in light and dark blues. Val didn't know exactly what to do. They didn't teach how to handle gallery openings in her six-week photography course. She tucked her hands in her pockets because, even though there wasn't anything around to be broken, she knew she would find something to break somehow.

"Val, hey." Dani approached from beside her. "Thanks for coming. I'm glad you could make it."

"Thanks for the invite," Val replied, turning toward her friend.

"Of course." Dani smiled at her. "Did you get champagne yet?"

"No, I just got here," she answered.

"Well, get yourself a drink. I have to make the rounds, but Peyton is over there with Lennox and Kenzie." Dani pointed at the wall opposite where they were standing. "Make sure you go over to say hello."

"I will. Thanks," she said.

Dani squeezed her shoulder and said, "You can really rock a tux, by the way." She winked at her.

After Dani walked off to talk to someone Val didn't recognize, Val found the waiter with the tray of champagne flutes, grabbed one, and headed over toward her celebrity friends. That was still so weird, she thought as she took a sip. She wasn't much of a champagne fan, but everyone else had a glass, and she wanted to look like she fit in a little.

"Val, hi," Peyton said, smiling at her. "Did you see Dani?"

"I did. She told me to come over here and say hi," she replied as if she needed a reason to talk to them.

"Glad you could come," Peyton told her with that thousand-watt smile growing even wider.

"Do you think we should leave early?" Kenzie asked her wife.

"He's fine, Kenz," Lennox said back to her wife, pulling her close against her side.

"Kenzie is still getting used to the whole leaving-your-baby-at-home-with-the-babysitter thing," Peyton explained.

"We take him on set with us," Lennox added. "And we still haven't found a full-time nanny."

"Because I don't want a nanny," Kenzie told her.

"That would be part of the problem, yes," Lennox said, laughing a little. "Babe, you're back at work now. You have fourteen-hour days all the time, and I'm working, too. We need to find someone to watch him when we're at work. It doesn't have to be when we're home. We also don't have to call them a nanny if it makes you feel–"

"Pretentious?" Peyton asked.

"Yes, thank you, Peyton. You're always so helpful," Lennox said sarcastically.

"Hey, Dani's job requires nothing these days since she just takes pictures whenever and wherever she wants. It's crazy convenient, and she loves it, but even we have a nanny because she can't always be there; and neither can I," Peyton said in Kenzie's direction.

"I know. We just waited too long to have him." Kenzie tucked her head into the crook of Lennox's neck. "I hate being away from him."

"That'll change," Peyton said, chuckling. "I love my brood, but sometimes, you just want to hang out with the adults. I'm very glad the trips are staying with us this week. I have three instant babysitters."

"What about that nanny?" Lennox asked.

"She's visiting her family in Reno. I do give people time off, Len." Peyton winked at Lennox.

Val just stood there with her head on a swivel listening to the back-and-forth between the old friends. She knew Kenzie and Lennox had waited a while to have their son, who was now at least a few months old; she wasn't sure how old exactly. She knew Peyton and Dani had two kids now. They'd had one right after the other. She also knew that Peyton had triplet sisters that she called the trips most of the time instead of by their individual names. Val just assumed that was easier or faster. It was almost like they were speaking a foreign language that she knew some of the words for and then had to fill in the rest using context clues. It was kind of like her Spanish class in high school. When she didn't know what the other words meant, but she knew 'baño' meant 'bathroom,' she could figure out the rest from there.

"Dani's work is amazing," Lennox said, changing the subject.

"It is, isn't it?" Peyton's smile was now a million watts again. "I'm so glad she's making this career change. When she was pregnant with Sienna, she was worried about if her body would be good enough after she had her. She worried about her diet during. She wanted to make sure she was eating right for the baby, but not over-indulging because that would make it harder to get back into model shape." She took a sip of her champagne. "Trust me, that woman's body is perfect. It has always been perfect." She laughed lightly. "Then, Dani started working out as soon as she could to lose the baby weight."

"The, like, ten pounds she gained?" Lennox joked.

"Ten pounds in the model world is like a hundred for everyone else, but yeah, I get what you're saying. And she actually likes working out because, of course, I married a crazy person." Peyton laughed again. "She still works out all the time, but now she only does it because she likes it, and she's not forcing herself into a routine."

"Her passion comes through in these photos," Lennox said.

"We bought one," Kenzie added. "But don't tell her. We want to have it framed and hang it up."

"It'll be a surprise when you guys come over next time," Lennox said.

"We're thinking about putting it on that wall that leads outside," Kenzie said.

"And maybe buying another one or two, but we haven't decided. We're thinking about making it the Dani wall."

"It's cool that she's donating all the proceeds to charity," Kenzie added.

"Well, it's not like we need the money; and she's just that kind of woman."

"Val, what do you think?" Kenzie asked her.

It was then that Val turned to Kenzie and recognized an expression on her face. Kenzie had noticed she was being left out and had made an effort to include her in the conversation. Val gave Kenzie a small smile that she hoped conveyed gratitude when, really, she kind of felt put on the spot. She still wasn't accustomed to the small talk and banter with this group.

"I like all of the ones I can see, but I just got here. I haven't walked around yet," she replied.

"We bought that one." Lennox pointed behind her and to the right.

It was a black-and-white photo with a small amount of muted color – as all of the photographs hanging up were – and showed a stormy sky. The sky itself was mostly various shades of gray, but there were some soft purples and pinks mixed in, giving it a surreal vibe.

"We're also thinking about getting the one next to it and maybe the other one hanging over there," Kenzie said, pointing at the photos in turn.

"It's kind of like they're a set," Lennox added.

The other two photos were the same size and also

showed mostly sky, but had a little tall grass mixed in there, too. In the first one, that tall grass had some soft greens and browns showing through. The final photo had a lake with various shades of blue and everything else around it in grays, black, and white.

"You know where she took those, right?" Peyton asked.

"No," Lennox replied.

"You really don't recognize it?"

"Should we?"

"Lennox, it's the lake," Kenzie answered for her. "We have to buy them."

"What lake?" Lennox turned to look at the photo again. "No way. That's *the* lake?"

"It's hard to recognize it in black and white," Peyton said. "But that's the lake, all right. She took those during our wedding."

"At the campsite?" Kenzie asked.

"Yeah, that's our lake, Kenz," Lennox said, smiling. "Well, it's more like a pond than a lake, I think, but that's it. That's where we had our first kiss. Well, our first several kisses."

"And the other one is that grass," Kenzie said, smiling as well. "You were freaking out about snakes." She laughed.

"I was not freaking out," Lennox argued.

"Yes, you were. It was so cute," Kenzie told her.

"We're buying them. Let's go find that guy we talked to before and pick them up before someone else does."

"You guys know she has copies, right? It's not like it's a painting," Peyton stated. "And she'd literally give you anything you want."

"Well, she's been holding on to these pictures for years, Pey. She didn't give them to us after she took them, did she?" Lennox gave her best friend a playful glare.

"She was a little busy announcing the fact that she was marrying me to the entire world, hiding out for months, having a lot of sex…" Peyton pointed at herself. "With me.

Oh, and then we got married. I went on tour a few times; she modeled around the world and then had our first kid followed by our second kid and is just now really getting into this, so… Please forgive her."

"Forgiven. But we're still buying them," Lennox said. "Let's go find him," she said to Kenzie.

They hurried off in search of whoever it was they were looking for, leaving Val standing there alone with the most famous woman on the planet.

"So, I like your dress," she told Peyton as she tried to search her mind for the next topic she could bring up just to have in her back pocket.

"Thank you. Dani picked it out," Peyton replied, smiling at her. "I guess it's from some designer she used to work with, and she asked for it specifically for me," she added.

"Well, she's got great taste," Val said.

"And you look good in a tux." Peyton looked her up and down. "Armani?" she asked.

"I don't know, but I doubt it. It's a rental," Val admitted. "I don't exactly have any reason to own one."

"Well, you're rocking it," Peyton said. "And if you're interested, there are at least two eligible ladies I know that I think would totally dig a woman who can wear a tux that well. One of them is here tonight."

"Oh, I didn't come here to–"

"What the hell is she doing here?" Peyton asked in a tone that was completely different than the one she'd had a moment earlier.

"I'm sorry?"

"Jessica fucking Morrison," Peyton said. "God, it feels good to swear. Now that Sienna is talking, we've got to be careful around the house; but fuck, it's nice to be out with people I'm not parenting." She nodded toward the door. "That woman broke Maddox's heart twice."

"Jessica?" Val turned around to see the most beautiful woman in the world standing in the open doorway, holding onto a small black-and-white clutch and looking around with an expression that told Val she wasn't exactly comfortable. "Jessica," she repeated.

"She's a cheating cheater. How did she even get an invite?"

"Cheating cheater?" Dani asked, approaching from behind Peyton. "You're way better than that, songwriter." She kissed Peyton's cheek as she wrapped her arms around her wife from behind. "And I invited her."

"You invited her?"

"I did," Dani said, letting go and moving to Peyton's side. "It is my show. I think I get to decide who gets to come, right? Besides, I don't know. I just felt like she was our friend, and it's time."

"Time for what?"

"To start letting it go, babe," Dani replied.

"Letting what go?" Val asked.

"That's Maddox's ex-girlfriend," Peyton replied.

Val had heard about Maddox's ex, but never by name. Sometimes, the friends had referred to her as Lord Voldemort. Other times, it was just 'the ex.' Val wasn't sure she would have put it together even if they had called her Jessica, though. The name was common. The woman it belonged to, though, was anything but common. She was drop-dead gorgeous and had Val swallowing hard just looking at her.

CHAPTER 5

"JESS?"

She knew that voice well and muttered a few curse words under her breath as she turned around and saw Maddox standing next to her girlfriend, Avery.

"Maddie, hey," she greeted.

"What are you doing here?" Maddox asked, moving the three of them into the open space due to the line forming at the door behind them.

"I was invited," she answered honestly.

"Dani invited you?"

"I don't know who invited me, Maddie. I just got the invite." Jessica glanced over at the other woman and said, "Hi, Avery."

"Hey, Jessica," the woman greeted and smiled at her, a genuine smile that Jessica was grateful for right now. "How have you been?"

"Good. How about you?"

"We're good," Maddox answered for her girlfriend.

"She means that we're both doing well. Thank you for asking," Avery said, tugging on Maddox's hand.

"Sorry. I just saw your face on a billboard driving over. I think I might still have some PTSD-like symptoms when I see you," Maddox said.

"I get it." Jessica nodded. "I should go. I made a mistake. I didn't think you'd be here."

"Why wouldn't I be here?"

She sighed and said, "Well, I stalked your social media feed, trying to see if you were in town, and if you were, I wasn't going to come. But you'd posted from Seattle, so I thought I wouldn't run into you and could just congratulate Dani and go."

"We just got back," Maddox said. "We were up there for a job for me, but Avery also had a couple of meetings with investors. We just landed a few hours ago."

"Well, I guess I could have texted to check, but I didn't know if you'd want that."

"Jess, you can text me. I'm not a total asshole. I'll reply."

"Okay. Well, now I know that if we're ever likely to be in the same place, I'll just text and ask if it's okay that I go."

"You know what?" Avery began, kissed Maddox's cheek, and let go of her hand. "I'm going to go find Dani and give you two a minute. I think you two should talk."

"Avery, we don't—"

"Maddox, I love you, but Jessica shouldn't have to text you to get your permission to come to a party her friend invited her to." Avery smiled at her girlfriend. "Work it out, babe. I'll be over there when you're ready."

Avery walked off to join their group of friends, leaving Jessica and Maddox standing off to the side of the door, not fully engaged in the party, but not exactly on the outside looking in, either.

"Well, I like her," Jessica said, breaking the tense silence.

"So do I," Maddox replied, laughing a little.

"Should I go, Maddie?"

"No, you don't have to go." Maddox sighed. "It's just my initial shock at seeing you coming out as rudeness. It happened at the last New Year's Eve party you showed up at, too. Sorry. You can go wherever you want, Jess."

"I got the invite today. I should have called Dani to make sure she actually meant to send it to me. Maybe I was on an old list she had or something, and it needs to be updated to remove former friends."

"I doubt it. It's Dani." Maddox shrugged a shoulder.

"True." Then, she took Maddox in for the first time. She was dressed in a pair of black pants, white shirt, and a black vest with a gray tie on underneath. "You look good, Maddie."

"So do you," Maddox said, looking at Jessica's dress. "I saw the movie is coming out."

"The premiere was the other day."

"Congrats. I hope it does well," Maddox replied and bit her lower lip. "I saw some stuff on TMZ from the red carpet. I noticed Lisa was there. Is that still a thing?"

"She's the costume designer," Jessica answered Maddox's unanswered question. "She signed on after I did."

"So, she wasn't there as your date?"

"I went solo," Jessica said, and then, decided to just tell the truth. That was the only way this could ever work. "Lisa and I had been on and off since the party, though; not in a relationship. We just–"

"Slept together?"

"Sometimes," she answered.

"Well, you're single. You can sleep with anyone you want." Maddox shrugged the other shoulder.

"We're not anymore. That's over."

"Why?"

"Because it's not what I want. It never was. I was just too stupid to recognize it before."

"What do you mean?" Maddox crossed her arms over her chest.

"That I'll never stop being sorry for what I did to you; to us," she said.

"Jess, we're at a gallery opening for Dani. We–"

"I know. It's about her tonight. I wasn't planning on seeing you, Maddie. I was planning on making my apology rounds with Dani and Peyton first. If Kenzie and Lennox were here, I'd try them, too. I was planning on working my way up to you."

"Hey," Dani said, walking over. "Mad, digging that thin tie on you. Those are in right now."

"Avery dressed me," Maddox said, still looking at Jessica.

"Well, she has good taste. Where is she?"

"She went to find you guys," Maddox replied, looking at Dani then. "Your stuff is amazing, Dani." She smiled at her.

"Not as good as yours."

"Don't make her head too big," Jessica said, laughing a little.

"My head is just fine," Maddox replied. "Seriously, though, it's great."

"Thank you," Dani said, smiling. "Peyton, Lennox, and Kenzie are over there with Val." She nodded behind Jessica, who was still looking at Maddox.

"My guess is Avery found the bathroom and is going over there after that. I told her to pee before we left, but she was busy apping."

"Apping?" Jessica asked.

"It's a word I made up. Avery created an app, and now she has this successful company. Whenever she can't stop taking notes or writing code, I call it 'apping.' It's cute," Maddox explained. "I should go find her and say hello to everyone."

"Sure," Jessica said.

"I'll see you later, Jess." She smiled a tight smile and walked off to find her girlfriend.

"Hey, Dani?"

"Yeah?"

"Why did you invite me tonight?" Jessica asked.

"Because I think it's about time, don't you?"

"Time for what?"

"You made a mistake, Jess. Well, you made a few of them, and they were really bad, but you're not a terrible person."

"Are you sure? Everyone here hates me," she replied.

"No one hates you." Dani squeezed her shoulder. "Peyton is still angry at you, yes. You hurt one of her closest friends. Lennox isn't your number one fan, but she's not someone that won't accept a heartfelt apology. Kenzie doesn't seem to feel any particular way about you, honestly. She just kind of vibes with whatever Lennox puts out about the whole thing. Even Maddox has warmed to the idea of a possible friend reunion."

"She has?"

"Well, she's danced around it the few times I've brought it up; but right after you two ended, she yelled at anyone who suggested the two of you could ever be friends, so I'm calling that progress."

"What about you?" she asked.

"You hurt one of my friends, Jess." Dani glared at her. "But I believe people can change and ask for forgiveness. I believe that you can earn trust back after it's broken. It just takes time."

"It's been a couple of years."

"And I forgive you for hurting my friend. Do you forgive yourself?"

"No," Jessica replied. "I don't think I ever will."

"Well, I can't do that for you. But I can invite you here. You should talk to Peyton. See if she's thawed on the idea."

"You know your wife. Has she thawed?"

"Not really." Dani laughed slightly. "But if I have, she will, too. It just takes her a little longer than me most times."

"Maybe I should wait another two years," Jessica said, giving Dani a look of concern.

"She acts like a pit bull, but she's a marshmallow."

"With you. You're her wife," Jessica replied, laughing a little.

"She's loyal, Jess. She doesn't understand how other people aren't sometimes."

"And I wasn't loyal to Maddie," she replied.

"No, you definitely weren't."

"Do you think Maddie will forgive me one day?"

"Honestly, I don't know. You'd have to talk to her about that. But I do think she's actually in a place now where she can hear what you have to say."

"She found someone." Jessica smiled. "I'm glad she has Avery. They make a sweet couple."

"They do. They bought a place together, and it wouldn't surprise me if a proposal is around the corner."

"Really?"

"Yeah, Mad is crazy in love, and so is Avery. It's pretty obvious that they're meant to be." Dani dropped the smile. "Sorry."

"Don't apologize. I lost her because I was an idiot. It's my fault. But, looking back, I don't think Maddie and I had a future. It seems like she was meant for someone else all along."

"That means that you are, too, though; and she's out there somewhere." Dani's smile returned. "Peyton actually invited someone tonight. I think she had the idea of hooking her up with our friend, Val, but–"

"Val?" That was the second time she had heard that name tonight, but the first time had been in a blur of words and emotions from seeing Maddox for the first time in over a year.

"Yeah, our friend Val. Have you met her? She's just over there." Dani pointed.

Jessica turned around, and that was when she saw the sexiest woman she'd ever seen, owning that tuxedo she was wearing.

"Venice," she muttered.

"You know her?" Dani asked.

"We've met," she answered.

"At the party?"

"Tonight?" Jessica double-checked.

"No, the New Year's Eve party. You were both there."

"We were?" Jessica asked, turning her head back to Dani but not wanting to lose sight of Venice, who was talking to another woman she didn't recognize.

"Yeah. I think you were there with Lisa, though, so maybe you didn't see her."

"I wasn't there with Lisa." She paused and shook her head. "Never mind." Then, she looked back at Venice and found the woman staring back at her. She offered Venice a shy smile but didn't get one in return. "She knows you guys."

"Yes," Dani said as if that was obvious.

"That means she knows what I did to Maddox." She lowered her head.

"If she didn't before, Peyton saw you come in. I didn't exactly tell the wife I'd invited you, so she said some things. Sorry about that."

"It's fine." Jessica lifted her head and turned back to Dani. "I should go."

"You can if you want. I won't stop you. But my guess is that you came here for a reason, and it wasn't to support my art."

"I did want to support you. I also wanted to start the apologies I owe all of you."

"Well, you did. You started with me. I've accepted your apology. Now, Kenzie was probably the next least affected. You should try her. Then, work your way up to Maddox."

"I'm more worried about Peyton than Maddox."

"Smart woman." Dani glared at her playfully. "Go if you want, but you've got us all in one room. Might as well try to go two for two."

CHAPTER 6

"WHY DID Dani invite her?" Lennox asked Peyton.

"Because she says it's time we all move beyond this. I love my wife, but I never thought we'd see Jessica again outside of the posters, billboards, and gossip sites that talk about who she's dating, deflowering, or otherwise turning gay."

"Turning gay?" Val asked.

"When two women in the business hang out, and one of them is gay or even bi, they all just assume they're sleeping together and that the gay one has turned the straight one a color of the rainbow. It's pretty disgusting if you ask me."

"It's fine, Pey," Maddox said. "She can be here. I don't hate her anymore."

"Well, I do."

"No, you don't," Maddox said. "And you shouldn't. We're all just trying to move beyond what happened."

"I'm going to…" Val didn't finish the sentence.

She didn't have to. The women were talking about Jessica as if she wasn't in the room. Granted, the room was huge, and Jessica was still talking to Dani by the door, so she couldn't hear them, but she needed to get away. There was something she didn't like about this conversation. She wasn't sure if it was because she felt like an outsider listening in, or because they were saying things about Jessica that she didn't like. Either way, she ran off to the bathroom; not to pee, but just to wash her hands and splash some water on her makeup-free face. One of the benefits of never wearing any, she thought to herself as she wiped her hands with the provided cloth and made her way back out to the gallery.

"Hi," Jessica said.

"Oh, hi," Val greeted.

She hadn't seen Jessica approaching from the side of the bathroom door.

"I didn't know you'd be here," Jessica said. "I swear, I'm not stalking you."

"No one has ever stalked me," Val joked.

"Well, maybe they should." Jessica looked her up and down. "You really fill out a tux."

"And you're a knockout in that dress," she replied.

"Thank you," Jessica said. "Listen, I didn't know you knew the people I know." She shook her head. "That came out wrong." She laughed at herself. "I just meant that I didn't know you were friends with Maddie."

"Maddie?"

"Maddox. Sorry, I call her Maddie," she said.

"Oh, well, I'm friends with Dani. That's how I met Peyton, obviously, and then I just met everyone else at that now-legendary party." Val hesitated. "I didn't know you knew them. I guess I should have assumed. Most celebrities probably know each other, at least in passing."

"But I don't know them in passing," Jessica said. "We were friends for a while."

"Were?"

"I know you know." Jessica shrugged her shoulders. "Dani told me that Peyton told you before I got the chance to explain. God, that sounded less complicated in my head than it sounded coming out of my mouth."

"Explain what?"

"What happened. What I did."

"To me?" Val pointed to her chest.

"Yeah. I didn't want you to – I don't know – find out that way."

"But you wanted me to find out?" Val asked, tucking her hands into her pockets.

Jessica watched the movement and said, "You look

really good standing like that; like an androgynous model."

Val removed her hands and hung them at her sides instead.

"Why would you need to explain anything to me?"

Jessica nodded and said, "I guess I don't. I thought–" She stopped and looked away. "Never mind. I don't know what I thought. You made yourself clear today and last night."

"Last night?"

"When I invited you to Wonderland, and you didn't show."

"You didn't invite me. You mentioned you were going and said I should stop by."

"Well, if this ever turned into anything, we'd definitely have to work on our communication." Jessica laughed.

"Turned into–"

"God, Venice, I've complimented you like ten times tonight already. I know you know I'm interested," Jessica said, giving her a pleading look.

"In me? Why?" she asked, moving aside for a woman who needed to get into the restroom.

"Look at you." Jessica motioned to Val's body with an open palm. "You're sexy as hell, and you don't even know it. Plus, I liked our conversation at lunch yesterday. That's why I was so hopeful you'd join me for a drink last night."

"Hey, I thought you were coming back," Paula said, walking up to Val.

"You did?" Val asked.

"I told you I had to make a call, but I'd be right back. Peyton told me you went to the bathroom, but I thought you'd join us when you got done."

"Apparently, I am aloof on all fronts today," Val said.

"I know you. You're Jessica Morrison," Paula said to Jessica.

"I am. And you are?"

"Paula Wright. I'm one of Peyton's producers," she said.

"Nice to meet you," Jessica replied and took Paula's hand to shake.

"You too." She stared at Jessica and then turned to look at Val. "Are you joining us?"

"Yeah, just a sec, okay?" Val said, suddenly feeling like she was stuck between a rock and a hard place.

"Sure," Paula said, looking at Jessica as if she were a culprit in some crime.

Then, she walked off.

"She seems nice," Jessica said once Paula was out of earshot. "Is she your date?"

"No, I just met her," Val replied. "Peyton introduced us."

"She's at it again, huh?"

"What?"

"Peyton. She likes fixing people up." Jessica nodded to the side toward the group of women. "You're looking at some of the results."

"Oh, I don't know if she specifically planned on us getting together or anything."

"Trust me; she did." Jessica crossed her arms over her chest, holding the clutch in her hand over her breasts. "Well, that puts it to rest, then."

"I'm sorry. I feel like I'm asking a lot of questions here. I don't like feeling like an idiot. Can you fill me in on whatever I appear to be missing?" Val crossed her arms over her chest, mirroring Jessica's posture.

"Peyton told you I cheated on Maddox."

"She did."

"And she's trying to set you up with her producer."

"I guess."

"And Paula knows how hot you are."

"Wait. No, that's—"

"So, it's settled. I'd planned to stop by the store tomorrow to try to ask you out on an actual date, and be very clear with my intentions this time, but that's a moot point now."

"Jessica, you were going to ask me out?" Val dropped her arms to her sides before feeling pretty good about herself and tucking them back into her pockets.

"That's not fair." Jessica looked down at Val's hands and then back up to her eyes. "Do that for Paula, but don't give me the sexy pose that I won't get to stare at all night."

"And to think, I didn't even want to come here tonight," Val said.

"You didn't?"

"I came for Dani because I wanted to support her work. I didn't come to be hit on by Paula."

"Or me?" Jessica asked.

"I had no idea you'd even be here. And yeah, I'm still a little confused as to why you'd be interested in me. You're Jessica Morrison." Val pulled a hand out of her pocket and motioned to her with an open palm. "You can have any woman you want."

"Except you, is my guess." Jessica let out an exasperated sigh. "I'm going home. This was a bad idea. I thought I'd be able to get back what I'd lost, at least in part. I'll take Dani's forgiveness and go home to wallow. It's a start. I'll try to take the win." She looked at the group of friends and then back at Val. "Have a good night, Venice."

"You don't have to go," Val told her.

"It's better if I do. I'm walking around with a big scarlet letter A on my chest." Jessica motioned the letter over her dress. "I'm not wanted here. Like I said, I hope you have a good night. Tell Paula to retract her claws. Hester Prynne is heading home." Jessica turned and walked away.

Val watched as she passed several people and gave them smiles. She even posed for a picture with someone before she finally left the gallery. Val walked back over to the group of old friends and some new ones.

"Hey, everything okay?" Paula asked her.

"Everything's fine." Val nodded.

"Did she leave?" Maddox asked Val.

"Jessica?"

"Yeah."

"She did, yes. I guess she didn't feel very welcome," Val replied.

Maddox gave her a solemn nod, looked at Avery, and said, "It's not my fault. I told her she could be here."

Avery rolled her eyes at her girlfriend and asked, "How have you been, Val?"

"Good. You?"

Avery was her favorite of the group. She would never tell anyone here that, though. Avery had been the other so-called 'average' or 'normal' at the party that night. It was true that Val had tried to pick her up, hoping they could go out and see if anything would come of it, but now, over a year later, Avery was a good friend, and that was enough for her.

"I'm great. I secured the funding I needed to expand," she replied.

"Congratulations," Val replied.

"Thanks."

"Lots to celebrate tonight," Peyton said, winking at Val and then nodded toward Paula.

"I was actually thinking about going for a drink after this," Paula said, looking at Peyton first and then over to Val. "Anyone interested in joining me?"

There was nothing inherently wrong with Paula Wright. The woman was probably in her late thirties. She had auburn hair and fair skin. She was a little shorter than Val, but only by an inch or so. She had been a good conversationalist when Peyton had introduced them, but there was just something preventing Val from being enthused about this clear setup by Peyton.

"I have an early shift tomorrow, so I was just about to head out," Val said.

"Really?" Peyton asked.

"Yeah, I have to open and do inventory before the morning rush."

"There's a morning rush at a pack and ship store?" Peyton asked.

"Yes, Peyton," Val said through gritted teeth. "There's a morning rush."

"Okay. I didn't know that."

"Anyway, tell Dani congratulations for me. I'll text you later," she said that last part to Avery.

"Sounds good. We should have lunch soon. We're in town for a while." Avery leaned into Maddox's side.

"We'll set something up." Val smiled. Then, she looked at Paula. "It was nice meeting you."

"You too," Paula replied. Then, she added, "Peyton has my number. If you're interested, give me a call."

"Thanks," she said, not knowing what else to say to that. If she said she'd do that, Paula would be waiting for her call. If she said she wasn't interested, the woman would be embarrassed. "Goodnight." She waved at her friends, nodded at Paula, and then turned to go outside.

She passed Dani on the way out, so she stopped and turned, waiting for Dani to wrap up her conversation with a man who was asking her questions about the photograph on the wall in front of them.

"Hey, are you leaving?" Dani asked her.

"Yeah, I just wanted to say congratulations. You're incredibly talented."

"Thank you." Dani smiled at her. "And thanks again for coming."

"Can I ask you something?"

"Shoot."

"Do you have Jessica's address?"

CHAPTER 7

WELL, last night had gone well. Jessica laughed to herself as she sat in the back of the studio-provided black SUV and waited to arrive at the station. She was up far too early for her liking, but it was all part of the job. The interview at six in the morning would reach the entire US and would help boost the movie, which she not only wanted but needed to do well. A lot was riding on its success. It was a gritty drama with few light moments, and she'd stretched herself far to play this character. People had been talking about awards, and that was just what Jessica needed. Not the trophies; she didn't care about the actual awards. She just wanted to be taken seriously. Many models had tried their hands at acting in the past. Very few of them had made careers from it, and some of the ones that had, hadn't ever been taken seriously for their films or shows. Jessica wanted to be different. She didn't want to be just a pretty face anymore. And if this movie did well, according to critics and audiences alike, she might just be on her way to achieving her goal.

The interview went fine. Jessica did the phony-smile thing, trying to make it look real, when she wanted another cup of coffee and to sleep another couple of hours more than she wanted to have to be smiling at this interviewer. She felt like she answered the questions they had agreed upon in advance with ease and even subverted the one tossed in by the male co-host about her relationship status. She had changed the subject and asked about his. He'd laughed it off, and they changed the subject back to the movie and her future plans. She'd given the stock answer:

she was reviewing scripts. It was true. She did have a pile of scripts to read through, but she was also okay with not rushing into the next movie or offer. Jessica wasn't sure exactly what she wanted yet. She did know that she didn't want to just sit around her house after she finished all this press. Maybe she would take a long vacation; spend some time in Europe. She could hide more easily in some of those cities than she could in Los Angeles. There was the cabin in Aspen and the apartment in New York City, but she would be easily hunted in New York, and Aspen in the spring and summer wasn't nearly as much fun as Aspen in the winter. She could go to Paris, though; spend a few weeks in one of her favorite cities. She'd have to go incognito if she stayed there, though. Too many people would recognize her.

When Jessica got home in the late afternoon, after a lunch interview with Entertainment Weekly and a short photo shoot for their cover, she was exhausted and ready for a nap. She got the email the moment she locked her front door. She clicked on it, not expecting a package, and wondering why, yet again, the delivery service could not manage to get through the security gate to drop it at her door like they had a thousand times before. They must have hired a new guy or something. Apparently, the package was already back at the station. That was weird. According to Venice, the drivers finished their routes and then brought things back, but this notice said it was already at the North Hollywood store. Jessica didn't know if Venice would still be there, but she figured it was worth a shot. She still had no idea what was in the package, but she was getting a lot of scripts now that the buzz about the movie was positive. Maybe some new intern or PA didn't know the procedure of having a courier drop them off either at the door or, more preferably, with Jessica's overpaid agent.

She changed out of her interview clothes and into a pair of skinny jeans, tan flats with a matching belt, and a white peasant top. Then, she placed her large dark shades over her eyes and headed to her car. Traffic was heavy, which was common for the time of day, but it was driving Jessica crazy in an uncommon way. She used her phone, even though she shouldn't have while driving, to find out what time the store closed. Google told her it was open until eight, but that didn't mean Venice would be there until eight. If Jessica was dealing with this traffic, she at least wanted to see the woman. She didn't care what was in the damn package. This was a second chance to say hello and maybe apologize for her abrupt departure last night. It was also a chance to find out covertly if Venice had gone home with that annoying and very obviously interested Paula woman.

She street-parked about two blocks away and walked hurriedly toward the shop, leaving her head down just in case. She did not have time for a fan sighting right now. She rushed to the door and then slowed, not wanting to seem like she was in a hurry. Then, she pulled open the door and walked into the store. There were two customers being helped at the counter by a young woman Jessica didn't recognize. She pretended to look through the office supplies on the side wall until both of them left. Then, she walked to the counter.

"Can I help you?" the young woman addressed her.

"I have a package that I need to pick up," she replied, looking around the behind-the-counter area.

"Sure. Do you have a tracking number?"

"I do." Jessica held up her phone.

The woman typed something into her computer and said, "Can you hold on a second?"

"Is something wrong?" Jessica asked her.

"No, I just need to grab my manager," the woman replied.

"Okay." Jessica looked at the woman, confused.

She wasn't sure if Venice was the manager, or if she was but wasn't the only manager. She waited as the woman disappeared into the back and returned moments later alone.

"I'm taking my break now, but my manager will be right out to help you."

"I'm sorry. What's the problem, exactly? I just got this email that told me to come get my package."

"She can help you," the young woman said.

"Don't be rude to the poor girl. I told her I'd take care of it," Venice said as she emerged from the back.

"Venice," Jessica said with a smile.

"Shawna, you can go on your break now."

"Cool. Thanks. I'm going to grab a smoke outside the Starbucks. Do you want anything?"

"No, I'm good. Jessica?"

"What?"

"Do you want anything from Starbucks?"

"No, I'm good," Jessica replied, a little taken aback by the question.

"I'll be back in ten."

"Make it fifteen," Venice told her.

"Cool. Thanks."

She disappeared into that back room again, leaving them alone in the store.

"So, I just came to pick up a package," Jessica said, lying through her teeth.

"I know. I'm the one who sent it," Venice replied.

"You sent me a package?"

"I did." Venice walked back to the pile of packages on another counter. "I asked Dani for your address, but she refused to give it to me; something about your privacy." The woman turned and winked at Jessica. "I had to wear her down just to get your email address." She picked up a tall, somewhat thin box. "Then, I had to kind of hack the system. I used your name and email, obviously, but the store's address, and sent the package here, so you'd get the notification. I thought you'd come by tomorrow, honestly." Venice placed the box on top of the counter between them.

"I was curious," Jessica admitted. "I wasn't expecting anything else."

"Well, it's not shoes if that's what you're thinking." Venice laughed a little.

"What is it?"

"Open it," Venice said, passing her a box cutter.

"Okay," Jessica replied.

Then, she slid the box cutter down one side of the taped box and then the other. She folded the long side of the box down to reveal a bouquet of yellow and white roses inside a clear vase. Jessica pulled out the arrangement and looked at Venice with a shocked expression on her face.

"My roommate works at a flower shop. I asked her to put it together for me."

"It's beautiful," Jessica told her, leaning forward to smell the flowers.

"White and yellow roses," Venice said. "I guess the white ones mean new beginnings, and the yellow ones mean kind of the same thing and friendship. I don't know. Flowers and their meanings kind of confuse me. Sometimes, one flower means, like, twelve things." She chuckled a little at her joke.

"You got me flowers?"

"I would have had them delivered to your place, but Dani wouldn't budge. I could have asked someone else, but – I don't know – it just seemed easier to do it this way."

"Why?"

"Why was it easier, or why did I get you flowers?"

"The last one," Jessica said.

"It seemed like you had a rough night last night."

"I've had a lot of rough nights, but it's not anything I didn't bring on myself."

"I don't know the whole story." Venice leaned over the counter. "I'm sure it's a long one, but – I don't know – I just thought I could do something nice for you, and maybe it would make things better for a minute."

"Venice, this is more than making things better for a minute. This is like making things better for a full year, the way my personal life has been going."

"Then, I'm glad. I don't know… Should I be glad? That doesn't sound great."

"This was very sweet," Jessica said, placing her hand on top of Venice's on the counter, feeling the softness and warmth of it, and looking up to meet the woman's dark eyes. "Thank you."

"You're welcome," Venice replied.

"When do you get off?" Jessica asked.

"As often as I can," Venice replied, winked at her, and then laughed.

"Well, that's good to know," Jessica replied.

"When Shawna gets back from her break, I'm taking off."

"Are you maybe interested in grabbing a coffee at that Starbucks?"

"Where would we put your flowers?" Venice asked, giving her a sexy smile.

"They can sit on the damn table. It's not every day a woman buys me flowers. I want to show them off." She leaned over the counter next to Venice.

"You got what the yellow ones mean, right?"

"What?"

"The flowers? Yellow means friendship."

"Yeah, I got that. Why–" Jessica then stood up straight as she realized, and said, "Ah."

"I just want to–"

"No, I get it. You heard about what happened between Maddie and me, and… Yeah, I get it. I figured that out last night."

"That's not what I was going to say, Jessica."

A customer entered the store and headed straight for the counter with a medium-sized box.

"I should get going. I need to get these into some fresh water," Jessica said, picking the vase up off the counter.

"Jessica, hold on a second, okay?" Venice looked behind her. "I'll be right with you, sir." Then, she met Jessica's eyes. "Let's grab that coffee. We can talk."

"It's fine." Jessica shrugged, pulling the flowers to her chest, breathing them in. "This really was sweet of you, Venice. Thank you. I needed something good to happen."

"Jessica, don't just walk out right now."

"Excuse me. I just need to drop this off. Can I get my receipt?" the man said from behind Jessica.

"I was just leaving," Jessica said.

"Hold on." Venice grabbed a business card from the tray next to the computer, wrote something on the back of it, and passed it to Jessica. "That's my cell. Just call me or text me."

"Why?"

"Why not?" Venice asked.

"I'll see you around, Venice, also known as Val." Jessica turned to leave.

"Venice Valentine Russo," Venice said.

Jessica turned back and asked, "What?"

"My full name is Venice Valentine Russo."

"My full name is Bruce Edward Billings. Now, can I get my receipt, please?"

CHAPTER 8

V AL had probably messed up. The truth was, she didn't know what, if anything, she wanted with Jessica Morrison. The woman was beautiful. Those hazel eyes, when trained on Val, were weapons that shot straight to her heart; and to some other key parts as well.

Val was worried, though. She didn't want what Peyton had told her and what she'd heard about Maddox's ex – not knowing it had been Jessica all along – to cloud her judgment of the woman. That wouldn't be fair. But, at the same time, Val didn't know if she could trust someone like Jessica with her heart.

"Hey," Devin, her roommate, said as she flopped down on the sofa next to her.

"Hi. How was work?"

"Boring," she said.

"You always say that."

"It's always boring." Devin shrugged.

"Are you going out with Jana tonight?"

Jana, Devin's girlfriend of nine months, worked for the city government in some job Val didn't quite understand. It did, however, typically give her the weekends off, which meant Devin would be staying at her place since Jana lived alone in a much better location.

"Yeah, she's picking me up. I wanted to talk to you about something, though, before she gets here."

"Okay."

"You know Jana is forty-two, right?"

"Yes, I am aware." Val laughed at the strange question.

"And I'm thirty-seven; not getting any younger."

"Devin, out with it."

"She asked me to move in with her, and I said yes."

"Oh," Val replied.

"I love her, Val. After my divorce, I didn't think I'd find anyone I'd want to be with again, and then she walks into my life and sweeps me off my feet. I want to really start our life together, and so does she."

"I think that's great," Val replied honestly.

"You let me move in here when I needed a place to stay during the separation and after the divorce was finalized. I will always be so grateful, and I love living with you."

"I know. But it's time for you to move on."

"You're good if I move out, right?"

"I'm good. I can find another roommate."

"You could also find your own girlfriend and move in with her or have her move in here."

"Well, if I did find a girlfriend, I don't think we'll move in together within the next three months, and that's about the amount of time I can afford to go without a roommate here with what I have saved up."

"I'll pay half the rent until you find someone," Devin offered. "I won't be paying rent at Jana's place. I can afford it."

"I can't ask you to pay rent when you don't live here, Devin," Val replied, smiling at the offer. "I'll be okay. There are plenty of people in LA looking for roommates. I was one of them once. I found this place when Tiffany lived here. Then, I took over the lease when she left, and you moved in. It's fine. I'll find someone."

"Don't use your savings if you can help it, though." Devin leaned in. "You're saving for the store, Val. If you can't find someone when the next month's rent is due, you tell me. I'll help out."

"I'll keep you posted." Val smiled wider. "And I am very happy for you two."

"Thanks. I hate moving, but I can't wait to move in with her. Her house isn't crazy extravagant, but it's nice, and she owns it. She was able to pay for it with the inheritance she got when her grandfather died, so there's no mortgage. She said if I wanted to, I could use the spare room as my office and finally write that great American novel I've been dreaming about writing since forever. Working at the flower shop is boring, and after a year of putting bunches of different-colored plants into vases and tying them up with ribbons, I need something else."

"You could go back to teaching."

"I know, but the ex is still at my old school, and nowhere else is hiring right now. That's why I got the job I have now, to begin with."

"You're certified to teach high school and college. Maybe try something at a university."

"That's even harder to get into. But, yeah, I'll look again. Until then, though, my sugar mama girlfriend said I could even be jobless for a bit if I needed to focus on my writing. She really is amazing, Val."

"I know." Val looked toward the door when she heard the knock. "And she's here."

"We're going out to celebrate the move. Do you want to join us?" Devin asked, standing up.

"I don't want to be a third wheel."

"Not possible. Come on. I'll buy you a drink."

"No, I'm good. I need to start posting for a new roommate anyway," Val said, smiling at Devin to let her know that she really was okay with her leaving.

"Okay, but I'm vetting whoever takes my place. I don't want you living with some psycho."

"Go. Celebrate with your sugar mama." Val laughed.

Devin left with Jana, who stopped in just to say hello to Val before giggling her way down the hallway with her soon to be live-in girlfriend. Val laughed at how fully grown adult women could giggle at the idea of moving in together. Then, her phone rang. She'd left it on the kitchen counter hours ago. She walked over, picked it up, and stared at the unknown number on the screen. Normally, she didn't answer unknowns, but she was bored, so she figured she could decline the credit card offer and waste a little time in the process.

"Hello?"

"Venice?"

There was only one person outside of her family that called her that, and she had all of their numbers.

"Jessica?"

"You can call me Jess. Most people do."

"Okay. Jess." Val smiled as she sat back down on her sofa. "Hi," she added a little more softly.

"Hi. Is it okay that I called?"

"I did give you my number," Val replied.

"I know, but I kind of left it a little vague… I wasn't sure if you'd be pissed off. You got me those beautiful flowers, and then I walked off without letting you finish saying whatever it was you wanted to say. I've been chastising myself ever since. I'm sorry."

"Well, that customer wasn't exactly helpful," Val teased.

"He just wanted his damn receipt," Jessica replied, laughing a little. "What man doesn't want a receipt and the love of a good woman?"

"A gay man, probably."

They laughed together.

"So, what are you doing right now?" Jessica asked.

"I had the day off, so naturally, I'm doing nothing. You?"

"I'm in New York, sitting around my apartment."

"New York?"

"Yeah, for the movie. I have a few interviews over the next couple of days. Then, I'll be back."

"How is it going?"

"It's fine. I'm tired of answering the same questions all the time, but it's part of the job."

"How about some different questions, then?"

"What?" The woman on the other side of the line chuckled, and Val liked making Jessica laugh.

"Where are you from, originally?" she asked her.

"Oh," Jessica replied, still laughing. "Here. Well, not here, as in New York. Here, as in LA; where you are. I'm a native."

"Me too."

"Yeah, I feel like it's pretty rare to find an LA native these days."

"Agreed." Val paused. "Where did you go to school?"

"PV. You?"

"Here. North Hollywood. You went to public school?" Val asked.

"I did. Is that so surprising? Palos Verdes Panthers all the way, baby."

"You were a cheerleader, weren't you?" Val laughed.

"No." Jessica laughed, too. "I had to drop out pretty early on."

"You did?"

"Yes. I got my GED when I was sixteen. I was just gone all the time, so traditional school didn't work for me."

"College?" Val asked.

"No," Jessica replied. "You?" she asked.

"Yeah, but it's a bachelor's degree in philosophy. So, it's not worth much," Val admitted.

"You're a philosopher?" Jessica asked in a tone that led Val to believe the woman liked the idea of that.

"No, I couldn't pick a major, so I just landed on that one. I'm a manager at a pack and ship store. That's where we met, remember?"

"Technically, yes, but we might have met at a New Year's Eve party a little over a year ago."

"But, we didn't."

"Maybe we did. Maybe I was in line waiting for a drink, and you were standing behind me, or maybe you were out by the pool, and I was walking past you."

"I was out by the pool for a while."

"Yeah?"

"Yeah, I found Avery and hit on her there."

"You did?" Jessica laughed.

"Yup. Then, Maddox walked over and claimed her." Val laughed then. "I backed off after that. Well, sort of. I managed to find her later, and we talked for a bit. I kind of thought about trying again, but she was already lost in Maddox land."

"They're good together?" Jessica asked.

"I'm sorry, Jess. I didn't think about—"

"No, it's fine. I'm not still hung up on Maddie. I want her to be happy. She deserves it for everything I put her through. And I don't really know Avery, but she seems good for her."

"She is."

"Good. That's what I want. I want her to have everything she wants."

"And what about you?" Val asked her.

"I don't deserve everything I want," Jessica said softly.

"Jess…"

"I don't mean for you to pity me. I've made all my own mistakes, and I'll spend a long time trying to make up for them."

"Do you want to talk about it?"

"I don't know." The woman sighed. "If I tell you the whole story, you might hang up, and I don't want that."

"What if I promise not to hang up?"

"Do you have two hours?" Jessica laughed again, but it was forced laughter this time.

"I have all night if you want," Val told her.

"I guess I should start at the beginning then," Jessica said.

"Good. I'd like to hear the whole thing from you instead of the random comments I've heard since meeting Maddox and Peyton."

"You're actually giving me the benefit of the doubt?"

"I usually do with people," Val said.

"That's a nice change of pace for me." Jessica sighed. "I guess I'll start with meeting Maddie." There was a pause where it sounded like she took a drink. "I fell in love with her instantly. When we went on our first date, I thought this was the last first date I would ever go on because I'd found the love of my life." The woman paused again. "We were together for only a couple of months before one of us had to go away for a job. I don't actually remember who left first, but we knew it was real enough to make it work even with our hectic schedules. It was okay for a while. We had all of those firsts you have as a couple. They all felt magical to me, and I wanted all the firsts to be with her. But then, we had to spend a full month apart. I think it was actually five weeks in total before we got quick twenty-four hours together because I'd worked it out to have a long layover where Maddie was working. It kept on like that for a while, and it felt like forever to me. Then, I met Lisa."

"Lisa?"

"She's a designer. I worked with her on a show and a shoot for her upcoming line. It wasn't at all how it was with Maddie. There wasn't instant love or, really, any love at all. Lisa was nice and clearly talented, and she was into me. This was right around the time it started getting harder and harder to get Maddie on the phone. In the beginning, we'd had nightly phone calls and morning text messages even if we didn't talk during the day, but that didn't last long. Suddenly, she was too tired to talk at night, and I just felt so alone." Jessica paused to take a drink again. "I've honestly never felt so lonely. I had a beautiful girlfriend with whom I wanted to spend the rest of my life with, but I was all alone. Wherever I was traveling, I was alone. There were other people around, but none of them were her. At first, we tried to line up our schedules whenever we could, but then it seemed like I was the only one making an effort. I'm sure it felt that way to me, but she felt that she was the only one. I don't fault her for that. I just know how it felt the third time we had tried to see each other, and she had taken a job elsewhere instead. It cut me like a knife, Venice. I felt an actual knife slice into my heart." She sniffled a couple of times. "Then, there was Lisa. She was attractive, and she'd been hitting on me pretty aggressively for months. I was lonely and stupid, so I said yes."

"Yes, to what, exactly?"

"At first? It was just a cup of coffee where I complained about my absent girlfriend. Then, it was drinks at a bar where I continued to complain about my absent girlfriend."

"And then?"

"It was her hotel room where I stopped complaining about my absent girlfriend and let someone who wanted me, show me how much," Jessica answered.

"How'd it feel?" Val asked, moving the phone from one ear to the other.

"In the moment, it felt good. I'm not talking about the orgasm; I'm just talking about being wanted. I liked that Lisa wanted me when Maddox seemed to be more concerned about her career and not trying to make us work. It also felt good, if I'm being completely honest, because it felt like I was getting back at Maddie for not paying enough attention to me; like I was a toddler trying to show my mom my new toy, and she wasn't interested." Jessica sniffled again.

"Do you want to stop?"

"No, I'm almost done. It's better to just go all the way through it." The woman paused. "Lisa and I got to know each other, and it was nice. We slept together whenever we saw each other for the next few months, and it always felt wrong. The wrong always weighed heavily on me. No matter how good it felt in the moment, it still felt wrong. The guilt continued to mount up, and finally, it all came crashing down. Maddie found out, or I told her; I don't remember, honestly. The whole experience is still a blur to me. I know there were fights and tears, and she told me she hated me. I cried a lot after that but not because of what she said; because I had been the one to bring it on us. It took some time, but I kept at her. I asked her; begged her for forgiveness. I'm not sure if she actually forgave me, but she did take me back." There was another sniffle. "It was a bad idea; us getting back together. Maddie's career was blowing up, and mine was kind of on the way down; at least, the modeling part. She kept getting busier. I kept getting jealous of her job and the fact that she spent so much time doing it that she had nothing left over for me. There was another woman who was interested. One night, she kissed me out of the blue. And I won't lie; I did kiss her back. It stopped there, and I didn't kiss her or see her again. I still did it, though. And I told Maddie. We fought again, and she dumped me again. Then, I tried and tried to get her back because I am incapable of taking a hint." Jessica sighed. "It took a while, but then I decided I was ready to see her again. I thought we could talk. I could apologize again and maybe get some closure. That was the night of the party."

"What happened that night?" Val asked.

"They didn't tell you?"

"They did, but I was hoping you would."

There was a moment of silence before Jessica said, "I tried. Maddie wasn't interested. I didn't get it back then, but I do now. To hear something like that, you've got to be ready and willing, and she wasn't at the time. Lisa showed up unexpectedly. I hadn't seen her in a while, but she was single, and I was single. We'd both had a few too many and decided to go up to one of the guest rooms. I thought that was a good idea, for some reason. I won't even attempt to blame the alcohol; just my own idiocy." The woman laughed a self-deprecating laugh. "We burst into the room only to find Maddie and Avery lying on the bed, talking. It didn't go over well. I was just about to…"

"You can say it," Val said when Jessica faded out.

"I was about to fuck Lisa; it wasn't just another random woman. She was the reason Maddie and I had broken up."

"Was she?"

"Was she, what?"

"Really the reason you'd broken up?"

Jessica sighed again and said, "Maddie wasn't exactly happy I'd slept with another woman for months, Venice."

"I guess I'm not thinking about it like that," Val replied.

"Well, how *are you* thinking about it?"

"Sleeping with another woman was the effect. What was the cause? You loved Maddox. You wanted a life with her. Had you ever cheated on another girlfriend before?"

"What? No. This was the first and last time," Jessica stated.

Venice allowed herself a small smile and replied, "So, why did you do it? What caused you to cheat?"

"I was lonely."

"And you thought having sex with someone that wasn't your girlfriend was the way to fix that?"

"You're really just going for the jugular right now, aren't you?"

"We don't have to talk about this," Val said, shifting the phone to the other ear again before she stood up. "What time is it there?"

"After eleven," Jessica replied.

"When do you have to wake up tomorrow?"

"Five."

"You should be sleeping, Jess."

"Probably," Jessica said. "But I'd rather be talking to you."

"Even if it's about your ex-girlfriend?"

"You said you wanted to be friends. This is what friends do, right?"

"It is," Val answered and pulled a bottle of water out of her fridge. "But you don't have to tell me your entire life story in one night."

"What are you doing?" Jessica asked.

"Getting something to drink." Val opened the bottle.

"I'm having red wine. What are you drinking?"

"Water." She chuckled. "And just how much red wine have you had so far?"

"Just one glass. I'm on my second, technically. Do you have any there? You could drink with me."

"I don't." Val took a drink of her water. "You should get some sleep."

"That's what the wine is for, Venice," Jessica replied.

Val laughed and said, "Cut yourself off after this one."

"You're not the boss of me," the woman said playfully.

"Do you even have a boss?"

"I do. Her name is Carol, and she's my assistant."

Val laughed again and asked, "Your assistant is your boss?"

"She bosses me around."

"Aren't you paying her?"

"To boss me around, yes," Jessica said. "Carol's great. She takes care of me."

"Can I have her number? I'd like to tell her to make you get some sleep."

"She's on vacation."

"Oh, that's why you're off your leash," Val joked.

Jessica laughed and said, "Yes. She comes back on Monday. She'll put the shock collar back on me and make sure I eat three square meals a day, I promise."

Val moved back to the sofa with her water and said, "Good. You clearly need it."

"Hey, can I ask you something?"

"Yes."

"It's what, around eight there?"

"Yeah," she said.

"Are you doing anything tonight?"

"I already told you, I–"

"I mean tonight, Venice. Like, after we hang up; are you going out?"

Val smiled and said, "No, I'm in for the night."

There was a minute of shared silence. Val waited for

Jessica to say something because she didn't know what to say herself.

"I thought maybe you'd be going out tonight," Jessica said finally.

"Why would you think that?"

"Paula," Jessica said.

"Ah, Paula Wright," Val replied.

"Don't tease me," Jessica said.

"I'm not." Val chuckled. "I'm not going out with Paula."

"Tonight? Or, ever?"

"Not tonight, and I can't predict the future."

"Venice?"

"Yeah?"

"I know you know I like you."

"I know you know I don't know why."

"Do you really want to just be friends?" Jessica asked and then sighed. "If you tell me that's what you want, I'll stop flirting with you or asking about your potential love interests. If you feel something more than friendship, though, can you just tell me? You can say it's not going to go anywhere. I get it. Most people think once a cheater, always a cheater. I would just like to know if I'm crazy for thinking that there's something here between us. I've felt it since I saw you in the store that first day, and it just seems like something worth pursuing to me; but I need you to tell me otherwise."

Val bit her lower lip, took a long drink of water, and then cleared her throat.

"I'm going to say a lot of things right now, I think."

"Okay?" Jessica asked more than said.

"I do feel it; what you're talking about. It's there, Jess."

"So, I'm not crazy?"

"No, you're not crazy. It's there," she repeated.

"But?"

"However," Val corrected.

"Don't use word trickery on me, Venice Valentine,"

Jessica said.

Val laughed and replied, "However, I do think we should just be friends."

"Why?"

"Not for the reason you think."

"So, you're not turned off by the fact that I cheated?"

"I'm not a big fan of it, to be honest. Although I don't have any relationship baggage from an ex-girlfriend who cheated on me or anything like that, I just don't like the idea of being with someone and giving them your heart only to find out that they'd given at least parts of themselves to someone else."

"I understand," Jessica said, sighing.

"But, that's not stopping me."

"Then, what is?"

"A couple of things, I think."

"Tell me."

"Well, you're a freaking supermodel-turned-actress, probably living in a Hollywood mansion. I manage a pack and ship store and have to find a new roommate to help with expenses because my current roommate just told me she's moving in with her girlfriend." Val paused. "I'm almost thirty-six, and I still have a roommate. You're my age and have houses all over the world, probably."

"I have three; but that's not the point, is it?"

"No, it's not. We're from different worlds, Jess."

"That didn't stop Maddie and Avery."

"Maddox is behind the camera. Most people don't stop her on the street for photos. She's not being stalked by paparazzi because she has a new movie coming out."

"You're friends with the most famous women in the world."

"I'm not dating them," Val replied.

"Now that would be a story," Jessica said, laughing lightly.

Val laughed as well and said, "I don't fit into your world. I didn't even fit in the art gallery. I just stood there like a deer in headlights. They were talking about things I have no way to relate to. Lennox had a hair and makeup artist come to her house to help get her and Kenzie ready just to go to a gallery opening. I rented a tux."

"Oh, you have no idea, do you?" Jessica said.

"About what?"

"Venice Valentine, if you were even remotely interested in modeling or acting, you'd be on the A-list, babe." Jessica paused for a moment. "You are seriously the sexiest woman I've ever seen, and it's even better because you really don't even realize how good-looking you are. You had that short hair slicked back with that tux on, and those hands in your pockets like you were about to walk a red carpet, and I was…"

"You were what?"

Jessica took in a deep breath and said, "Ready."

Val shifted in her seat, swallowed hard, and asked, "Ready for what?"

"You." Jessica must have taken another drink. "For you to do whatever you'd want to me; for me to touch you everywhere you would let me. I just… I was ready."

"Oh," Val uttered because she had nothing else to say.

"We should change the subject." Jessica cleared her throat this time. "I'm getting turned on just thinking about it, and I have to go to sleep soon."

"Wait. Really?"

"Venice, unless you plan on having phone sex with me right now so I won't be all hot and bothered during my interviews tomorrow, you'll tell me the other reason why you don't think we'll work."

"Other reason?" Val shook her head, trying to remember, but the mention of phone sex and Jessica Morrison in the same sentence had her brain all scrambled. "Oh, yeah." She let out a deep breath. "I don't know that you are."

"Are, what?"

"Ready for me."

"Is that a challenge?" Jessica gave a daring laugh.

"I'm not talking about sex, Jess."

"What are you talking about, then? All I can think about right now is sex, so you're going to–"

"Why did you really sleep with that Lisa woman?"

"Venice…"

"The feelings; the reasons you did that; that's what caused your relationship with Maddox to end. I don't know. I just feel like you need to sort through that stuff."

"And, what? You'll be waiting on the other side after I do?"

"That's not what I'm saying, and I'm not telling you to do anything. It's your life. They're your feelings. I can't tell you to do anything with them, and I wouldn't even if I could. I don't know what's going to happen if you are able to sort through them, but I can tell you that I can be your friend while you do."

"Friend?"

"Yes."

"My friend that I talk to about phone sex?"

Venice laughed and said, "We can talk about whatever you want."

"But, you won't be the friend I have phone sex with?"

"Haven't you done the friends with benefits thing already? I thought you wanted more."

"I do. You're right," Jessica replied. "I think I should get some sleep."

"Cork that wine, Jess. Tomorrow night, if you want, you can pour yourself a glass and call me again."

"Will you have wine with me?"

"I'll go out and buy some tomorrow for the occasion."

"It's a date, then," Jessica replied.

Val decided to let that go and said, "Good night, Jessica."

"Night, my sexy friend."

Val laughed and then disconnected the call.

CHAPTER 9

"So, anyone special in your life?" the interviewer asked.

"I have a lot of special people in my life," Jessica replied, lifted the coffee mug filled with water to her lips, and took a drink she didn't really need.

"No lady in particular, though?" he asked.

"I'm single if that's what you're asking."

"There were some rumors going around for a while that you were dating Lisa Grandy. Any truth to them?"

"Lisa is a friend. And she was a costume designer on the movie, but we're not together." Jessica put the mug back down and wished she could glare at him without the live studio audience seeing it, but the camera focused in on her, made that impossible.

"How was it, working on the movie? It was your first as a lead with a pretty well-known director."

The subject change without a segue; this part of the interview, Jessica was used to. As she delivered the same token line her publicist had given her, she thought how, at this point, she had probably said the same thing about fifty different ways to over a hundred interviewers and reporters. She even wondered how people didn't get bored of hearing it as they tuned into multiple entertainment shows. The interviewer, one of late night's most popular hosts, showed a clip from the film, asked her a couple more questions about it, and the interview was over.

She unclipped her microphone in the greenroom, took a long drink of her coconut water, and unbuttoned the top two buttons of her evergreen silk blouse. It had been a long day. This was the second talk show interview of the day, but she'd also had an abbreviated press junket that morning in a hotel close to her apartment. She'd had thirty-two interviewers asking her questions for six minutes apiece. Those were the same three or four questions every time, and Jessica remembered what her agent had told her when she first started modeling. Well, he'd said it more to her mother than to Jessica, but she remembered it, nonetheless. He'd said that the way he could tell if someone was cut out for this industry, was if they could do the same thing over and over again and not get irritated or annoyed. Basically, could they hang in there when the photographer asked them to pose a hundred different ways for hours on end. Her ability to do that helped her acting career as well. She had been asked to deliver take after take in an identical way to get coverage and to film as many camera angles as needed. Then, she had been asked to do it three to four different ways so that the director and editors had options. Now, she had to answer the same questions as if her iPhone was on repeat, playing the same song over and over. She had to smile and pretend like she hadn't just answered all of them two minutes before, but she managed to get through that, and then her final two interviews in New York.

She'd opted to stay the night and fly back the following morning. Jessica didn't care for the red-eye and didn't own her own plane like Peyton, so she'd be subject to whatever flights were going to LA like everyone else in the world. Since she also had her own apartment here, she didn't see the point in scrambling to get home. She'd leave tomorrow, at a decent hour, avoiding the rush hour traffic and allowing herself to sleep in a little more than usual.

When she got back to that apartment, she showered off the makeup and hair spray, choosing to slide into some silky pajamas that she had loved so much, she ended up buying a pair for each of her homes and one extra in LA. This pair was all black, and it was so soft, she loved just touching the fabric; it soothed her. She uncorked a bottle of wine after she finished the dinner she had had delivered, and poured herself a glass. It was a big glass. Jessica didn't want to have to get up for a refill later.

Then, she went into her bedroom and climbed into bed. It was way too early for her to go to sleep, but she wanted to be comfortable. She reached for her phone and, stalling because she was nervous, she scrolled through her social media. She hit the little thumbs up and heart icons a few times and posted something generic about how much she loved being in New York City on Twitter. Then, she posted a photo of Times Square on her Instagram. She made sure to mention the name of her movie and its opening date in each post. After that, she had nothing else to do to stall. She dialed Venice's number, put the phone to her ear, and waited.

"Hey," Venice said moments later.

"Hi," Jessica replied.

"Done for the day?"

"Yeah. You?"

"Yeah. I just got home, actually. Devin wasn't kidding when she said she was excited about moving. I worked a half-day at the store and then helped her get some of her things out of the apartment and over to her girlfriend's house."

"That was nice of you," Jessica said, smiling just at the sound of Venice's voice. "Do you need some time to settle in or, I don't know, take a shower?" She bit her lower lip at the thought of a naked Venice in the shower.

"No, I'm okay. Just let me grab some water, and I'll go into my room."

"Your room?"

"My bedroom."

"It's early there."

"I know, but the living room is now filled with half-put-together boxes, tape guns, and a bunch of random shit that Devin is taking with her; so, it's better in my room."

"How long have you known Devin?"

"Probably about five years."

"How'd you meet?"

"Through friends we had in common at a party one of them had."

"Did you two ever date?"

"Devin and me?" The woman laughed. "No, we never dated. We'd be a terrible couple."

"Why's that?"

"Well, for one – and if you ever meet her, you can never tell her I told you this – but Devin's a fan of older women with money. She is older than me, and I don't have any money."

"And her current girlfriend?"

"Is about five years older and has enough money so that Devin can technically quit the flower shop if she wants."

"Nice," Jessica said, taking a drink of her wine.

"How was your day?" Venice changed the subject.

"It was fine. I had, in total, about thirty-four interviews."

"Thirty-four?!" Venice exclaimed.

"It's the press junket. It's usually longer, but I had to cram it all in today, so I only did about half as much as I normally do."

"I don't know how you do it."

"I don't know how you do your job."

"Packing and shipping things?"

"Working with customers, managing employees, managing an entire store, and whatever else goes on there."

"It's not that big of a deal."

"I can feel you shrugging through the phone," Jessica said with a smile on her face.

Venice laughed and said, "Yeah, yeah."

"What are you doing tomorrow?"

"Working," Venice said.

"And, after work?"

"Nothing that I know of. Devin said she'd have the rest of her stuff out by tomorrow. Jana – that's her girlfriend – is hiring movers for the big stuff."

"Come over," Jessica said without thinking.

"To New York?"

"I'm flying back tomorrow morning. Come over to my place."

"Your place?"

"Where I live, Venice." She laughed. "I have a home, you know?"

"I'm sure you do," the woman said, laughing as well. "Okay."

"Yeah?"

"Sure. Should I bring anything?"

"A bathing suit," Jessica said.

"A bathing suit?"

"Well, I assume you don't want to skinny dip."

"No, not really." Venice laughed again. "I'm not much of a swimmer, though."

"You live in Los Angeles."

"And I don't go into the ocean."

"What? Why?"

"Because I'm not much of a swimmer," she repeated.

"Are you afraid of the ocean?" Jessica asked her.

"I'm afraid of sharks, jellyfish, and the fact that I never took swimming lessons as a kid, so I don't want to get caught in some riptide and carried out to sea."

"There are no riptides in swimming pools," Jessica said, unbuttoning the top button of her pajama top, feeling a little warm all of a sudden. "Just me."

"You may very well be a riptide, for all I know," Venice replied.

"I won't carry you out to sea, Venice," she said softly. "Just come over for dinner. I'll cook us something."

"You cook?"

"I read. Carol, it turns out, left me recipes for a few things in my junk drawer. She could have easily emailed them, but no. They're written by hand and waiting for me when I get home. She has this chicken dish she makes for me sometimes that's really good. I could make that for us."

There was a moment of silence. Jessica worried she'd gone too far. Maybe asking the woman to come over to her place was too intimate, given the still constant flirtation between them even after Venice made it clear that she wanted them to just be friends. She couldn't exactly just invite the girl out for a meal, though. One of the reasons Venice was hesitant, to begin with, was that Jessica was famous – especially now, with the movie coming out. If they went out, and Jessica got spotted, it might spook Venice from even wanting a friendship with her; and she didn't want that.

"What time?" Venice asked.

"Seven."

"I work until six. Can I come over dressed how I am?"

"You can wear whatever you want." Jessica reached to unbutton the next button of her shirt. "I may be wearing a bathing suit, though. I've been missing going for a swim recently."

"Bikini?" Venice asked.

"Always," Jessica said, unbuttoning the next button.

"You're mean."

"Am I?" she teased.

"Yes, you know you are."

"I know I only own bikinis, so it's either that, or I'm swimming naked. Which would you prefer, Venice?"

"Those are my only two options?"

"Yes." She laughed a little.

"Well, my actual preference, if I'm being honest, is that you're naked."

"Yeah?" Jessica unbuttoned the final button and spread the soft silk back, revealing her breasts to the cool air in the apartment.

"Yes, but you knew that." The woman paused, which gave Jessica enough time to use her free hand and squeeze

74

her left breast. "I told you there's something here last night."

"You did. I remember," Jessica replied, moving a finger and thumb to her own nipple and playing with it, wanting to make it hard so that she could feel it against the silk. When it peaked, she pulled the shirt back over it and squeezed her breast through the shirt. She then bit her lower lip and said, "But you also said you just want to be friends."

"Jess, wear the bikini before I get there. Then, put on a parka or something before dinner."

Jessica laughed a little and replied, "I do not own a parka."

"Then, a trench coat."

"Only a trench coat?"

"Jessica…" Venice grunted a little.

Jessica pulled the other side of her shirt over her right breast but left it unbuttoned. Then, she made sure just enough of her cleavage was showing before she took a picture.

"Hold on," she said and then sent the photo.

"What? Why?" There was a moment of silence. "Did you just send me something?" There was a pause again. Then, Venice said, "Jesus, Jess."

"What? I'm not naked," she replied with a smirk only she could see. "Besides, if you're that turned on by the thought of me being in a bikini, this is good practice for you."

"You look sexy," Venice replied, a little huskier than before.

"Are you still looking at it?"

"Yes," she answered.

"Do you want another one?"

"No," she replied instantly. "For starters, I couldn't take it. Secondly, you'd probably lose the shirt, and the first time I see you topless will not be in a picture taken from your phone. Also, celebrities get hacked all the time. You need to be careful."

"I've posted worse than that on my social pages. I'm a model, Venice." Then, Jessica realized something. "You just said, the first time you see me topless won't be in a picture."

"Yeah, I guess I did," Venice stated and seemed to realize at the same time.

"Does that mean you plan on seeing me naked?"

"It means, I can see your nipples through that shirt. What is that? Silk?"

"Yes," Jessica replied, separating the shirt again, and looking down at her chest. "And the buttons are undone all the way; in case you're curious."

"Are you doing what I think you're doing?"

"Not yet," she teased.

"Fuck!"

"That's the idea," she said.

"Jess, this is not how friends behave."

"And I told you that if you really wanted to be friends, I would honor that, Venice. But you said that's not the case."

"I also said there were reasons we shouldn't be more."

"Well, I can't remember those right now. What I do remember is you looking sexy as hell in that tux, and me wanting to rip that bow tie off you, tear the shirt open, and then take–"

"Okay. Okay. Slow down," Venice interrupted.

"Gladly," Jessica replied, sliding a hand inside her panties. "First, I–"

"No, Jess. I don't mean, go slower with what you're doing. We're not having phone sex right now."

"Well, one of us is."

"I thought you weren't."

"I just started."

"You're going to kill me. I am actually going to die knowing that," Venice said.

"You could be a part of it," Jessica told her, cupping herself, not touching anything in particular yet.

"Not tonight. This isn't right, Jess."

Jessica pulled out her hand and asked, "Why not?"

"Because if we ever do this, the first time is not going to be over the phone."

"How will it be?" Jessica folded her shirt over her chest.

"It won't just be because we're turned on or because we haven't gotten laid in a while; that I know for sure," Venice said.

Jessica slid her hand out of her panties and asked, "Are you a romantic, Venice Valentine?"

"My name didn't give it away?"

"Your parents named you."

"True. But, Jess, let's just talk tomorrow night, okay? I'll come over after work. We can talk about what this actually is between us, because I don't know if it can be just friendship."

"Really?"

"I thought about you all day," the woman admitted softly.

"What did you think about?"

"That I love talking to you. I don't know why, but I do. I liked talking to you at the restaurant the other day, at the shop, and even at the gallery, despite the fact that it was crazy awkward. I know I don't just want to talk to you as a friend."

"How do you know that?"

"Because I know I don't want to be the one you talk to about some woman you met and are going out with next week."

"Try being me with Paula Wright." Jessica took a drink of her wine.

"Nothing is going to happen with Paula."

"Is anything going to happen with us?"

"I don't know. But if it is, it won't be when we're on the phone. Come home, okay? We'll talk."

"I'll swim before you come over. I'll be showered and appropriately dressed by the time you arrive."

Venice chuckled and said, "I'll bring the wine I bought for tonight but haven't actually opened yet."

"No, open it. Let's keep talking and drink together like I was there."

"Fine, but no more pictures and definitely do not touch yourself while we're talking," Venice said.

"I cannot promise either of those things." Jessica smiled at her own words.

CHAPTER 10

"THANK you," Val told the customer who handed her the package that she then scanned. "And here's your receipt."

"Thanks," the woman said and turned to go.

"We're all moved out," Devin said as she entered the shop. "Well, I'm moved out, but Jana helped. I brought you a coffee." She placed the cup on the counter.

"Thanks," Val said. "To what do I owe the honor of my now ex-roommate's presence?"

"I just put in my two weeks' notice down the street. I decided to celebrate with coffee for myself, for Jana, and for you. The ones for Jana and I are in the car. So is she. I shouldn't stay too long, but I wanted to stop by and thank you."

"You act like I'm never going to see you again." Val slid the coffee cup toward herself.

"You'll see me all the time. We have that party next week. Jana and I are going. Want us to pick you up?"

"No, I'm good. I'll be there."

"Okay. How's everything else?"

"You mean this?" Val motioned around the empty store.

"You have more in your life than just this store," Devin told her.

"Not really." She shrugged.

"You have a friend that knows your coffee order. That's something." Devin winked and then rubbed her arm over the counter. "How much do you have saved? When can you buy your own place?"

"I have enough for the franchise fee, but I'd still need to find a location, lease the building, and then cover the build-out. I'm still a couple years off, I think. I actually have an appointment at my bank in about an hour just to check in and see if I'm right."

"Can I ask you something?"

"Sure." Val took a drink of the coffee.

"You've been talking about owning one of these places since you became a manager."

"Yes, I have. What of it?"

"Well, whenever you talk about it, there's never any excitement there. It's just like a thing you're going to do, but it doesn't seem like it's something you actually want to do."

"I want to be my own boss. Right now, I work for the guy who owns the place. He's fine, but if I owned my own store, I could tell people I own my own business."

"And that's important to you?"

"I am almost thirty-six, Dev, and I work in an office-supply, pack-and-ship hybrid store. I'm salary, so I guess that's something, but when I look at what other people my age are doing with their lives, it just makes me feel about three inches tall."

"Who cares about other people, Val? If this place makes you happy, you can work here until you retire. If you want your own shop because it's what you really want, then that's great, too. But don't compare yourself to everyone else. I work at a flower shop, for Christ's sake. I'm not even the florist. I just work there, taking orders and helping with arrangements she tells me to make."

"Not anymore," Val replied.

"That's true. I am very lucky. But even when I was teaching, I knew I was only doing it because I thought I should be. I majored in English education, but that was because I was too scared to major in creative writing. I'm older than you, and I'm only just now getting it together."

"You were married, at least," Val argued.

"And look how that turned out." Devin chuckled. "I

met her at the school we both worked at. We became friends, dated, and then got married. It all seemed fine, taking the car together to work each day and night. Then, she started going in earlier and making excuses to stay later. She didn't even tell me. I had to find the TA on her knees in front of my wife, who was leaning on the desk like she was the happiest woman in the world."

"I'm sorry you had to go through that."

"There wasn't a chance in hell I could work there after the divorce, and I also needed a career change. I found something temporary. Wasn't this supposed to be temporary for you, too?"

"It was, but it's not terrible."

"You're bored." Devin pointed at her just as she got a text on her phone. "You're bored. Admit it." She checked the phone. "That's Jana. She's double-parked, so I have to go. But, admit it to yourself, and think about what you really want to do with your life, Valentine." She pointed at her again. "And you don't look so good. Are you okay?"

"I was up late last night," Val replied.

"I repeat: are you okay?" Devin took a few steps backward.

"I am. I was on the phone with someone for a while."

"Who?" Another text message came in.

"I'll tell you later. Go. Your girlfriend is waiting," Val said as she laughed at her friend's antics.

"I'm going to marry her, Val." She smiled the widest, happiest smile Val had ever seen on her. "She's the one."

"I'm glad. I'll be at the wedding. Or, in the wedding; whatever you want."

"Maid of honor has a nice ring to it," Devin said as she waved and left the shop. "You'd look good in a tux," she yelled as the door closed.

"That's what they all say," Val mumbled under her breath to no one.

*****

81

"With the franchise fee, you're good," her financial advisor at the bank told her. "If you're looking to buy land, you've got a way to go, though."

"I'm going to have to lease," Val said.

"Right. To lease something in this area, depending on the exact location and the square footage, you could be looking at twenty to thirty thousand a month. It might even be higher. Some of these streets, there are shops not much larger than a Coffee Bean location that are forty a month."

"And getting a loan for that would be difficult, I take it?"

"Well, you don't have any collateral," the guy replied. "You don't own a home. Your car is yours, but it's—"

"Old?" Val guessed and laughed. "Yeah, I know."

"Your credit is okay; not great." He paused, looked at the computer screen, and then back to her. "If you had someone to co-sign with you, that could help. It would need to be someone with collateral or good credit, obviously, and they'd need to understand that if you couldn't repay the loan, they'd be on the hook for it."

"I don't have anyone like that," she said.

"Okay. Then, based on how much you're saving per month, and how much you'd need to be able to get the loan, I'd say you're looking at another two to three years, at least."

"That's what I thought."

"If you could put away a little more each month, that would shorten."

"I know," she said. "Thanks for taking another look for me." Val stood.

"Not a problem. It's what we're here for. When you're ready to get that loan, stop back by. I'd be happy to work on the paperwork for you."

***

"Hey," Jessica said with a smile when she opened the door to her giant home.

"Hi," Val said, feeling about three inches tall again. "This place is massive."

"You've been to Peyton and Dani's place, and you think this one is massive? They have at least three more bedrooms than I do. I don't have a loft or that game room, either," she replied. "Come on in."

"I brought you these," Val said, passing the box of candy.

"You brought me Sour Patch Kids?" Jessica asked excitedly.

"You said they were your favorite candy last night."

"I did." Jessica laughed and took the two boxes Val had brought. "I can't believe you bought me these. Thank you."

"I would have brought the wine, but–"

"You drank the bottle on the phone with me last night?"

"Yes, but also because the wine I buy isn't probably the wine you drink," she said, moving into the foyer, because yes, this place had a foyer. "It's one step above box wine."

Jessica stared at her and said, "I think you think I'm pretentious. Is that what you think?"

"No, I–"

"I'll have you know that the wine I was drinking with you was just regular old red wine. It was given to me in the greenroom that first day. I think it's about twenty bucks a bottle, probably, and it was fine by me."

"Okay." Val laughed and held up her hand. "Then, I should have brought the wine."

"No way." Jessica pressed the bright-yellow boxes to her chest. "I like this gift way more."

"I'm sure you have a bunch of them around here."

"Nope," the woman replied. "I only buy them every so often."

"Why? They're your favorite."

"I don't want to get sick of them," she said. "Now,

come on. Let me give you the tour." Jessica placed the boxes on the table by the door with the giant vase of fake flowers. "Oh, before I do that… How's my attire? Respectable enough? Do I need to cover more parts?" she asked with a smirk.

Jessica was wearing a black, sleeveless turtleneck shirt and a pair of skinny jeans with no shoes. She was wearing makeup, but only a small amount, and her long hair was pulled back away from her face. She was beautiful.

"No chance of you putting on a baggy T-shirt that is maybe covered in stains?" Val joked.

"Nope," the host woman said, shaking her hand.

"Then, I'll just say that you look beautiful and leave it at that."

"And I'll just say that you look sexy in that," Jessica stated.

"I'm wearing jeans and a button-down."

"Untucked, with a couple of wrinkles, and your hands are in your pockets." She pointed. "You look cool, and – I don't know – like you just don't give a fuck."

"Well, I assure you, I give many fucks," Val replied.

"Just one thing, okay?"

"What?"

Jessica walked up to her until they were only a foot apart. She reached for the top button of Val's shirt, which she always buttoned for work, and undid it. Then, Jessica undid the one under it, and Val wondered if she'd continue until all the buttons were undone, but she didn't. She took a step back and stared into Val's eyes.

"Better. Now, you look a little more comfortable."

Val trembled a little as she looked into those hazel eyes and said, "I don't feel more comfortable."

"What do you feel?" Jessica asked, tilting her head to the side.

"Like this isn't just two friends having dinner."

"That's because it's not," Jessica said.

"What is it?"

"Me trying not to repeat the mistakes of my past. Me trying to show you that this is something I want; that I don't just want to be your friend. It's a lot of things, I think."

CHAPTER 11

"YOU have an infinity pool?!" Venice practically yelled when they went outside with plates of food.

"I do. I told you I have a pool. I even suggested you bring your suit. You turned me down."

"You didn't say it was an infinity pool," she replied, turning back to Jessica.

"Would that have changed your mind?"

"No, but it's still cool."

"You hang out with the most famous women in the world, and you think my place is the coolest?"

"I don't hang out with them regularly," Venice said, sitting down next to Jessica at the patio table that faced the view of the pool and LA beyond it. "I see them every so often. I spend the most time with Avery, and her place with Maddox is pretty normal."

"Maddie likes that."

"What?"

"Normalcy," Jessica answered, taking a sip of the wine she had already poured and left out for them.

"You don't?"

"I do." She sat the glass down. "I guess I just like nice things, too. Maddie would wear the same shoes for years until they got holes in them, and then argue about replacing them because a new pair would be a hundred bucks. I'd just replace the shoes."

"Would you wear them for years, though? Don't you have a million pairs of shoes?"

"I'll have you know that I wear the same pair of tennis shoes practically everywhere. I wore them the day we met, and I wore them home from the airport today," she said, lifting a defiant eyebrow at Venice.

"Do you think you guys would have worked if you–"

"Would've been faithful?" Jessica finished for her. "I don't think that anymore, no," she stated, taking a bite of her lemon chicken.

"Why not?"

"Well, she has Avery."

"But, she might not have met her if you two had stayed together."

"Maddie and me…" Jessica sighed. "She was stuck."

"Stuck?"

"Stuck between two worlds. I wasn't. I'd been in this one for a lot longer, and as much as it can be a pain in the ass, at times, I like it. I like my fancy house, even though it feels too big for just me. I like my infinity pool and my hot tub, and the view of the city. I like my nice shoe collection and designer clothes. I also like the work I do to earn them."

"And Maddox?" Venice took a bite and gave Jessica a smile. "It's delicious."

"Thank you." Jessica smiled back. "And Maddie was always the reluctant fashion photographer." She then took another bite and chewed for a moment as she thought about how best to describe her ex-girlfriend. "She was doing nature photography mainly until she met Dani at a show. She was talented; still is, but she wasn't making a whole lot of money back then. She still did weddings and new baby gigs to support herself, but she was a talent on the rise, as they say. Then, she met Dani, and all of a sudden, everyone wanted to work with her. She took a few shots of Dani in a nice dress, that Dani posted on Instagram later, and boom. Maddie was wanted by all the designers and magazines."

"You're saying she didn't want that?"

"I'm saying she took it, but Maddie loves nature photography. She always has. She likes the candid shots of people living their lives more than she likes the posed shots for magazines. I do think she likes fashion enough, but part of the reason she was never around when we were dating was that between fashion gigs, she'd take side jobs with other companies or magazines. National Geographic loves her. She's done a bunch of shoots for them."

"So, that's why you felt like she was choosing her job over you?"

"Hard not to when she actually did, don't you think?" Jessica replied.

"I can see that."

"The first time, I understood. The second time, I tried to understand. By the time she canceled on me for the third time, I had lost the ability to understand how someone I loved, and I thought loved me, would want to go take pictures in a forest instead of spending time with me."

"And you got lonely?"

"Maddie is amazing. I wanted that amazingness to surround me, but she feels that way about her art." Jessica paused. "And now, about Avery, I guess."

"Maybe they were just meant for each other, and that's why you and Maddie didn't work out."

"Well, the sex with someone else didn't exactly help."

Venice laughed and said, "I don't think so, no."

"I never should have slept with Lisa." Jessica shook her head rapidly from side to side, thinking back to that moment when Lisa was about to kiss her for the first time. "I knew it was wrong. I could have stopped it."

"But, you didn't. Why not?"

Jessica dropped her fork to the plate, turned to Venice, and said, "Because it felt so good to just be wanted, needed by someone else. I needed that then. I still need it now. Maybe it makes me a clingy partner or a co-dependent one. It took me a long time to figure out that I don't want someone like Maddie, who doesn't really need anything but a camera and a place to point it. I don't doubt that she loves Avery, but – from what I've heard about her – she doesn't need Maddie how I used to need her. They're perfect together and for each other because they can be apart. They can be independently working on whatever they want and not feel what I felt when Maddie was gone; when I just needed her to show up for me one time, and she couldn't." Jessica paused and looked out at the city skyline. "I hurt her because I couldn't be honest with her. I tried. I told her I needed to see her. I asked her not to take one gig and then the other, but I could tell it was important to her. I hurt her because I couldn't tell her how important she was to me and what that meant."

"What about the kiss?"

"The other woman?" Jessica asked.

"Yeah."

"That was me not being honest with myself. I loved Maddie, but I wasn't in love with her anymore. I'd begged her to take me back because I felt so guilty for what I did."

"And since?"

"Since what?"

"Since you guys broke up?"

"Who have I dated?" Jessica double-checked that she understood the question correctly.

"Yeah. Is that an okay question to ask?"

"No one," Jessica replied. "I mean, no one serious. I had a girlfriend for a while after Maddie and I had ended. She was nice. Things were okay for a while, but she was newly out and wanted to explore, if you know what I mean. It ended. Then, Lisa and I did the whole friends-with-benefits thing on and off. We weren't ever together, though. That's it."

"No one serious?" Venice asked, taking a drink of her wine.

"No." Jessica shook her head slowly as she looked at the beautiful woman sitting next to her. "I was kind of hoping there might be in my future, though." She gave Venice a soft smile.

"Oh, yeah?"

"Yeah… She's about five-eight, has this suave look about her, and really fills out a tux." She ran a hand through Venice's hair. "She's also totally into me but doesn't want to admit it."

That earned her a laugh, and Venice said, "She has admitted that she's into you, actually."

"She's also playing hard to get," Jessica argued.

"Maybe she just likes to get to know a woman before she goes all-in."

"Maybe I like that," Jessica said and then added, "that she's like that."

"That's good." Venice pushed her half-eaten meal away and leaned over. "Ask me about my relationships."

"I did last night. You told me about your ex-history."

"Ask me what I thought was missing," Venice said.

Jessica chuckled, feeling suddenly nervous, and asked, "What did you think was missing?"

"I've never had a girlfriend that just needed me," the woman replied.

Jessica swallowed and asked, "Never?"

"I have a degree in nothing that matters to most people, a pretty meaningless job, and no real money or a nice house. I've never really had much to offer, and the women I've dated all had more than they needed. They didn't need me, too."

"So, you're looking for a woman who needs you?"

"I wasn't." Venice looked at the view of the city for a second and then looked back at Jessica. "I'd given up on the whole thing, honestly. When I met Avery, I thought she was cool, so I struck up a conversation. But she, it turned out, was already taken. And it wouldn't have worked anyway, obviously. I haven't really tried since."

"And you're trying now?"

"No; that's the thing." Venice shook her head. "I'm not. You just showed up in my life and kind of turned it upside down. I'm not trying with you. I'm honestly just being myself."

"That's good, because I like you how you are."

"Even though I've worn a tux exactly twice in my entire life?" Venice joked.

"I'll buy you a damn tailored tux. You can wear it every

day or never again; I don't care." Jessica placed her hand on Venice's neck and stilled it there. "I haven't known you long, but I feel like I have. Is that weird?"

"No, I don't think so."

"What *do* you think?"

"That I don't have anything to offer you, Jess."

"What?" Jessica removed her hand.

"Did you not hear all of the things I don't have in that list I just rattled off?" Venice laughed that self-deprecating laugh she had.

"I don't care about what you don't have. I care about what you do have."

"What's that?"

"Whatever it is, it's what I've been missing," Jessica said honestly.

Venice looked toward the pool, likely to break the tension between them, and said, "Well, whatever that is, it's not the ability to swim." She laughed again.

"We can remedy that," Jessica said.

"No, we really can't." Venice leaned back in her chair. "You know how I met Avery at the New Year's Eve party by Dani and Peyton's pool?"

"Yeah…"

"I was praying that no one would push me into the thing. It was the only empty seat I could find outside, but there were people everywhere, and I was just hoping no one would push me in accidentally or on purpose, as some joke, because I would've been fluttering and spluttering around."

"Do you really not know how to swim?"

"I guess, the basics. I never took lessons or really learned, though."

"I'll teach you," Jessica said, standing up.

"What? No. I think the years where swimming would have been helpful are behind me."

"They don't have to be." Jessica held out her hand. "Come on, Venice. Trust me, okay?"

CHAPTER 12

DID Val trust her? They'd only just met. She probably shouldn't have, but she did. There was just something about this woman that told her she could trust her; that she wouldn't hurt her.

"I didn't bring a suit… And I am not skinny dipping with you, so don't even think about it."

"You could borrow one of mine."

"Yeah, no way that fits me, supermodel." She pointed at Jessica.

"You're wearing a bra and underwear, right? They cover the same real estate." The woman shrugged a sexy shoulder.

"You're just trying to get me out of my clothes." Val squinted at her.

"No, I'm not, but I'm going into the pool. If you want to join me, feel free. If not, I'll be awhile. I might go into the hot tub after. You'll have to entertain yourself."

Jessica pulled at her turtleneck until it was over her head, revealing a red bikini top.

"You're wearing your suit?"

"I didn't swim before like I said I would. I kind of hoped this would happen." She unbuttoned and unzipped her pants, causing Val's eyes to drop as she parted the sides, revealing the red bottoms beneath.

"Nothing is happening," Val returned.

"So, you're not checking me out right now?" Jessica teased as she slowly removed her jeans and hung them over her chair.

"I am totally checking you out right now," she replied. "But I'm not getting in that pool."

"I didn't say you had to, but I am."

Val watched as Jessica took a drink of her wine. Then, she walked that model walk, which had Val nearly drooling because the woman's legs were so long and toned and tan. Jessica was very tan, but not overly so. It made Val wonder if she was tan under the bikini, too. Then, she heard the jets in the hot tub turn on as Jessica twisted some knobs. Jessica made her way to the pool's edge, turned back around, smirked at her, and then dove into the pool, leaving hardly a splash of water behind her. By the time she emerged, Val had stood and walked over to the side of the pool.

"How is it?" she asked.

"It would be better if you joined me," Jessica said, splashing her lightly.

"Hey!"

"Babe, get in the water. It's only five feet deep. You'll be fine. I'm here. I promise, I will not let you drown."

"I shouldn't."

"Yes, you should. Get in here with me." The woman giggled.

Val hesitated before she kicked off her shoes and socks, which caused Jessica to start cheering her on. When Val started unbuttoning her shirt, the woman stopped cheering. She lowered herself almost fully into the water, leaving only those wicked hazel eyes above it, staring as Val undid each and every button. When Val pulled her shirt apart and slid it off her shoulders, she could have sworn she saw Jessica's eyes darken. Val normally wore a sports bra, so she didn't exactly feel sexy, considering her swim partner was the sexiest human alive. She unbuttoned her jeans, unzipped them, and let them lower to the ground before she picked them up, quickly tossed them over one of the empty chairs, and made her way to the steps at the end of the pool.

"Boy shorts are hot," Jessica said, turning her body to follow Val's movements.

"So are bikinis." Val took a few steps into the water, wanting to get beneath it as soon as possible, feeling a little vulnerable being almost naked with a Maxim Hot 100 model staring at her. "I'm just going to get in and stay close to the side, okay?"

Jessica slid in the water as if she'd been doing it for years. And maybe she had. She wasn't afraid of the pool.

"Come here," she requested softly, holding out her hands for Val to take.

Val took them and was pulled into the middle of the pool. A moment later, Jessica's arms were around her neck, and hers were around Jessica's waist, pulling her in. Then, Jessica's legs were around her body, and Jessica was above her, staring down at her, with wet lips that she licked, and an expression that told Val she didn't just want to teach her how to swim.

"I'm here," she said and swallowed.

"Yeah, you are." Jessica ran her hands through Val's still dry hair. "I like this."

"Me too," Val replied, running her hands up and down Jessica's back.

"Not afraid anymore?" Jessica asked.

"I think I'm more afraid than ever," she answered, but she wasn't referring to the water. "You're not going to teach me how to swim tonight, are you?"

"No," Jessica replied honestly. "But I will some other time."

"What are we going to do in here, then?"

"That's entirely up to you." The woman ran her hands through Val's hair again before wrapping her arms around her neck. "I like your bra."

"It's a sports bra," Val said, stating the obvious.

"I know. I like it," Jessica replied with a smile. "It suits you. Can you tell me something?"

"Maybe."

"How do you always manage to look so good to me?" she asked in a whisper as her face moved closer to Val's.

"I don't know." Val swallowed again. "You always look good to me, too."

"I think we should go with that, don't you?"

"Jess…"

"I need to kiss you now, Venice. Please let me. It doesn't have to go any further than that tonight, but I need to kiss you."

Jessica's lips hovered just above her own. Val stilled her hands on Jessica's back before bringing one to Jessica's cheek, cupping it, and bringing their lips together. Jessica's lips were soft and wet, and they molded to her own so much so that Val let out a little whimper, unable to control herself. Jessica let out a moan a second later. Then, her hands were in Val's hair, massaging her scalp. Val's hand cupping her cheek lowered to her hip and squeezed it. It was then that she remembered Jessica's legs were wrapped around her body. She ran her other hand to Jessica's ass and cupped it through her bikini bottoms.

Then, Val's tongue moved into Jessica's mouth, and Jessica's tongue joined it, twisting and swirling around Val's until Val needed to pull back to breathe. It didn't last long before Jessica pulled her back in. Val let her and sucked the woman's bottom lip into her mouth. Jessica's hands moved to her shoulders and then covered her breasts, pulling her own body back just a bit so she could cup them. Val moved her mouth to Jessica's neck, licking the skin and the chlorine that now coated it before she kissed and sucked. Jessica moved her hands back around Val's neck and gasped as Val sucked her earlobe into her mouth.

"God, this is what I wanted," Jessica whispered out.

"In a pool?" Val asked, teasing the earlobe with her teeth now.

"You. I can't get you off my mind. An interviewer asked me if I have anyone special in my life, and I swear I almost said your name."

Val pulled back to look up at her and asked, "You did?"

Jessica reconnected their mouths, sucking now on Val's lip. Her hips began to move against Val's abdomen.

Val moved her other hand to join the one on Jessica's ass to hold on to her.

"Yes, I did." Jessica kissed Val's cheek and looked at her. "I know this is crazy, but you're like a drug to me."

"That doesn't sound good." She kissed between Jessica's collarbones, wanting to place her lips under that bikini top and onto the nipples she felt peaking through it.

"It's pretty amazing. I haven't felt this in–" Jessica stopped, so Val looked up at her. "It's been a while."

Val smiled up at her and kissed her again. Jessica's hands went on the move again, trying to find any skin they could touch.

"We should slow down," Val said a few minutes later.

"Slow down? We're just heating up," Jessica replied, hopping off Val and pulling Val's hands until she had her own back to the infinity wall of the pool, and she had Val pressing her up against it. "Please keep kissing me."

Val gave her a soft smile and leaned in. They stayed there, in that exact position, exchanging slow, sensual kisses mixed in with some fast, heated ones until long after the sun had set. When Val looked up at LA, it was in the semi-darkness of after-dusk.

"We missed the sunset," she said as Jessica nibbled on her neck.

"We'll catch it next time. We're lucky: it performs daily around the same time."

Val laughed and then cupped Jessica's chin so she could look into her eyes.

"You're gorgeous," she muttered.

"So are you."

"I should go," Val said.

"You should stay."

"No, I should go."

"No, you should stay." Jessica pulled her into herself, pressing their bodies together. "The hot tub is more than warmed up for us."

"Another time, okay?" Val kissed her.

"Tell me what you're thinking," Jessica requested, running her hands again through Val's now somewhat wet hair.

"As much as I would love to stay, I think I should go home."

"Okay. Why?"

"Because I don't know."

"Well, that makes a lot of sense." Jessica lifted an eyebrow at her. "Is it because of your reasons?"

"Reasons?"

"The two reasons you gave me; why we shouldn't do this?"

"I guess. I think we're kind of already doing it, though."

"No, we're not. Trust me. You will know when we're doing it."

"Jess," she began, leaned in, and whispered, "You and I will not be 'doing it.' When we do that for the first time, we'll be making love."

Val watched Jessica smile a very small smile. She kissed her then, cupping Jessica's face in both hands, enjoying the feel of her in this new yet already familiar way.

"When will I see you again?"

"Got any new shoes you need to order?" Val teased.

"No, but I have this crazy amazing woman I'd like to spend more time with, and I'm hoping she'll agree to go out with me."

"Out?"

"I know you're not a fan of the celebrity thing, Venice, but I can't help who I am. Things are hectic with the movie coming out, but they'll die down. We can just have dates here if you want, or at your place. We don't have to go out."

"You think I'm worried about being out with you?"

"You said–"

"I said I'm not worthy. That was what I meant, Jess. I don't get how this Victoria's Secret Angel and movie star would want to date me. We can't have dates at my apartment. You'll end things the moment you walk into the place."

"Hey," Jessica said softly, placing her hand over Val's heart. "Stop making me seem like I'm a spoiled rich girl, please. That's not me. I've worked hard since I was thirteen for what I have. I don't apologize for that, but I also don't expect the woman I'm seeing to have what I have or want that, Venice. I wish you would stop selling yourself short and see yourself how I see you."

"How do you see me?"

Jessica smiled and said, "You are someone I could easily fall in love with."

CHAPTER 13

"THANKS for meeting me," Jessica said.

"Sure." Kenzie sat down across from her in a tiny, locals-only café hidden in Venice.

"Did you tell Lennox you were coming?"

"I tell Lennox everything," she replied.

"What did she say?" Jessica asked.

"Nothing."

"Really?"

"She was holding our screaming child at the time, so I think she had other things on her mind."

Kenzie looked around the room, which was small but had several customers in it. Some of them were likely staring at her. Kenzie lowered her eyes to the table.

"Well, thank you for coming."

"You said that already," Kenzie replied, looking up at her.

"Right." Jessica chuckled. She'd forgotten how direct Kenzie could be sometimes. "I'm trying to – I don't know – apologize to people I might have hurt for my terrible decisions in the past. I kind of started with Dani, and she suggested I keep going with you."

"You didn't hurt me, Jessica."

"I hurt Maddie, and you're friends with Maddie. So is Len."

"That's true." Kenzie nodded a couple of times. "Are you sorry?"

"Yes," Jessica replied honestly and sighed. "You have

no idea how sorry I am for what I did to her."

"Are you sorry because of what you did, or are you sorry because of what you lost because of it?" Kenzie asked a very pointed question.

Jessica leaned back in her uncomfortable chair and said, "Wow. I don't know that I've ever thought of it that way."

"Either you're sorry because of your actions, or you're sorry because of the consequences of them."

"But does it have to be *either*?"

"What do you mean?"

"Just that I don't think those things are mutually exclusive. I am sorry for what I did. I hate that I hurt Maddie like that. I still remember the look on her face when she found out. I'll never forget it, and I'll never forget that I caused it."

"Okay."

"And I'm sorry for what I lost, too. I lost Maddie then, but I would have lost her anyway. I get that now; we're not meant to be. But I lost my friends, too. You were one of them, and maybe not for as long as some of the others, but I'm sorry for what I lost because I miss you guys." Jessica felt herself tearing up. "I know I have no right to say that because I'm the reason everything happened, but I do."

"You can miss your friends, Jess."

"Well, that's good, because I do."

"Have you talked to Maddox?"

"She's toward the end of my list. I need to build up some more confidence before I try that again. She wasn't ready every other time I tried."

"She might be now," Kenzie said.

"Really? Why do you say that?"

"Hey, babe?" Lennox Owen walked into the café and stood behind Kenzie with a baby in a stroller. "I'm sorry. I was just going to walk him around the block, but he won't stop crying. Do you think you can get him to stop?" she asked.

Jessica looked down at the crying baby and then up at a slightly exhausted and worried Lennox. She wanted to chuckle at the new mom but thought better of it.

"Hey, Len."

"Hi," Lennox said.

"You talk to her." Kenzie stood up, bringing the baby with her. "He needs to eat, probably. I'll take him into the bathroom."

"I just—"

"Lennox," Kenzie said softly, using her free hand to cup Lennox's cheek. "Baby, just talk to her. Please."

"Okay," Lennox agreed.

"I forgive you, Jess," Kenzie told her. "For what it's worth, I forgive you." She patted Jessica's shoulder, used her free hand to then grab the stroller, and pushed it toward the bathroom as the baby's cries started to subside.

Lennox sat in Kenzie's chair and said, "She's such a good mom. I feel like I'm going to pull my hair out when he cries like that. She just picks him up, and it's fine."

"I'm glad you guys decided to have kids."

"Me too," Lennox said.

"How is he?"

"Liam? He's good. I'm a proud mom, so I can talk about him all day; or, we can talk about the reason you asked Kenzie here."

"Well, your very direct wife has rubbed off on you, huh?"

"That she has," Lennox replied, crossing her arms over her chest. "He latches on pretty quickly these days, so if you have something to say, you might want to say it before she finishes up in there."

"I'm making amends."

"You're an alcoholic?"

"No, Len." She leaned forward on the table, clasping her hands together. "You know what I'm apologizing for."

"Why are you apologizing to me; to Kenz?"

"Because I hurt your friend, and indirectly, I hurt you."

"You hurt Maddox. That's all I care about."

"I know. I'm no longer making excuses or blaming her, though, Lex. It was me. No matter what was going on in my relationship with Maddie, I shouldn't have slept with someone else, and I am sorry."

"Did you tell her that?"

"Most of it, but there's more I'd like a chance to talk to her about. I'm working on it."

"Well, work faster. She isn't getting any younger, Jess."

"I know." Jessica clenched her hands tighter. "I wanted to apologize to you first."

"Why me?"

"We were friends once, Lennox – you and Kenzie. Maddie came out to you both. Then, we hung out a little, and I thought we were all friends. Then, I fucked it all up."

"You want to be friends again?"

"I'd like to know that there's the possibility of being friends one day."

Lennox seemed to consider her answer for a long moment before saying, "Okay. There's a possibility of us being friends again one day."

"You need to talk to Maddie first, though, don't you?"

"I don't ask Maddox who I'm allowed to be friends with. She's not Regina George, and I'm not Gretchen Wieners. This isn't high school, Jess. I just need to think about it."

"Okay."

"Who's next on your list?"

"Technically, it's either Maddie or Peyton."

"Oh, do Maddox first. She'll be way easier than Peyton."

Jessica laughed and said, "I should probably apologize to Avery before them."

"Why? She wasn't around then."

"She was at the party when I almost got busy with Lisa."

"Oh, that's right. I always forget about that." Lennox

stood up when she noticed Kenzie coming out of the bathroom. "I don't think she needs an apology from you, but if you talk to her, she's going to tell Maddox, so you should plan your list accordingly." Lennox looked up at Kenzie then. "How'd it go?"

"He didn't eat. He thought about it for a minute and then passed out against my boob," Kenzie replied as she pushed the sleeping baby in the stroller over to Lennox.

"Like mother, like son." Lennox wiggled her eyebrows at her wife.

Kenzie glared at her playfully and asked, "Did you two play nice?"

"Yes, we did." Lennox took the stroller from Kenzie. "We should get him home before he wakes up."

"It was good to see you, Jess," Kenzie told her.

"You too," she said back.

"Jess, we're okay," Lennox said to her. "You and me; we're okay. Just don't do anything stupid like that again to anyone I care about."

Jessica thought about Venice but didn't say anything. She just nodded.

"See you around," Kenzie offered.

"He's adorable, you guys," Jessica said as they pushed him away.

"Like mother, like son," Lennox said again, nodding toward Kenzie.

Kenzie blushed, and then they were gone. Jessica sat in the café for a while longer. She hadn't ordered anything, though, and after about twenty more minutes, she was getting the eye from the barista. She felt bad, so she ordered herself a coffee. Then, she decided to do something nice. She texted Venice and waited for her response, hoping it would come sooner rather than later. As she finished her coffee, the response came in. Jessica walked back up to the counter and ordered another drink.

***

"Hey, you meant now?" Venice asked as Jessica walked into the shop.

"I did. When did you think I'd be bringing you coffee?"

"Your text just asked me how I liked my coffee. I thought it was a sex thing," Venice replied as Jessica placed her coffee on the counter.

"How exactly do you think I like my sex, Venice?" she asked, leaning over the counter.

"I meant, like a morning-after-sex thing; like you'd want to know for the future or something. I didn't think you were bringing me coffee."

"Well, I did. But I will also happily bring you coffee the morning after sex, too," Jessica replied. "Also, hello. And since we're alone right now, can I kiss you?"

Venice laughed, pushed the coffee to the side, leaned over the counter, and gave her a quick kiss.

"We're not technically alone. Nick is in the back. He's on break, so I'm watching the counter."

"When are you off? We could grab dinner."

It had been a few days since their time in the pool. Jessica had missed Venice, but she'd been busy with press and reading the scripts that continued to litter her table. They hadn't yet made plans for another date.

"I can't. I have this party thing tonight."

"Party thing? What exactly is a party thing? I've only ever been to a party."

Venice laughed a little and said, "It's a friend's party. I promised Devin I would go. It's someone's birthday."

"People still have birthday parties at our age?"

"It's his fortieth. His husband is throwing it for him since he's been struggling with the whole over-the-hill thing."

"Try being a supermodel. Over the hill is twenty-six," she replied.

Venice laughed again and said, "You seem different, somehow."

"I do?"

"Yeah, you seem happier or something."

"Well, I am happier. I'm here with you." Jessica leaned in again. "And I'm sneaking another kiss." She kissed Venice quickly and pulled back. "Is this party a plus-one kind of thing or…"

"Fishing for an invite?"

"Maybe." She placed her hand on top of Venice's.

"I doubt it's your kind of party, Jess. There will most likely be some carrots and celery in plastic, store-bought containers with also store-bought ranch dressing in a little cup in the middle. There will also likely be pizza rolls."

"And how do you know that's not my kind of party?"

"Jess…"

"Venice…" Jessica squeezed the woman's hand. "My kind of party is whatever party you're going to."

"That's sweet."

"I know." She winked. "So, it's totally okay if I can't go, but–"

"You can come with me."

"Yeah?" she asked excitedly.

"But, I'm picking you up in my shitty car."

"Great. I can't wait." Jessica pulled back. "I'm going home to find something to wear."

"Jessica, it's a casual thing; jeans and a nice shirt. Don't go crazy."

"I wasn't planning on it. I'm thinking the Oscar de la Renta gown I wore to the Emmys one year."

"Jessica…"

"I'm kidding. Calm down, Valentine. I'll see you later," she replied, suddenly feeling light on her feet and happier than she had been in a very long time.

CHAPTER 14

VAL was more than a little nervous, but she'd said yes to Jessica. She couldn't exactly take it back now. She pulled up in her old hatchback and buzzed the security gate.

"Hello?"

"It's me."

"Who's me?" Jessica asked.

"Jess, it's me."

"Me, who?"

"Really? Jessica Morrison, open this damn gate, or I'm going to the party without you."

She heard Jessica laugh, and then the gate in front of her opened. Val drove up to the house, parked, and got out of the car, watching as Jessica came out of the house wearing a cute little navy-blue and white sundress and matching flats.

"That was fun," Jessica said as she approached, holding her clutch in front of her.

"Ahoy, Matey! Where's the ship?" Val asked.

Jessica stopped walking immediately and got a scared look on her face.

"Do I look like I'm going to a boat party? It's the navy and white, isn't it? I should change. I don't want your friends thinking I dress like this all the time."

"Hey, come over here," Val said, smiling at her.

"Seriously, Venice, you have to tell me if I look ridiculous. This is not one of those traps. You will not get in trouble if you tell me I look ridiculous."

"Jess, you look cute." She put her hands on Jessica's waist and pulled the woman into herself. "I was just joking."

"I don't want to look cute. I should look, I don't know, like I fit in."

"Jess, you're a freaking movie star. You will not fit in

with my friends."

Jessica pulled back and gave her an expression that she couldn't read at first. Then, Val realized she was angry. Well, maybe not angry, exactly, but it certainly wasn't Jessica's happy face.

"I won't fit in?"

"I didn't mean it in a bad way. I just meant that you stand out, Jess."

"I don't want to stand out tonight, Venice. I want to meet your friends and spend time with you."

"We will."

"Do you want me to go?"

"Of course, I do." Val slid her hands a little lower, to Jessica's hips.

"You don't, though, do you?"

"Jess, what are you talking about?"

"You keep talking about how we don't fit because of me, because of my career; but it's you, Venice. You're the reason you think we don't fit."

"What's that supposed to mean?"

"That I have no problem with your job, your apartment, your car, or your friends. You do, though, and for some reason, you think I wouldn't want to be in your life when it looks the way it does. I do, but if you can't see that, I don't know what the point of this is."

"I've never dated a celebrity before, Jess. Can you cut me some slack?"

"Why don't you cut yourself some slack, Venice?" Jessica cupped her cheek. "Babe, no one's perfect; I should know. I like you. I think you and I could have something, but you have to believe that, too. Until then, I think I'll skip the parties."

"Jess, don't–"

"Why don't you call me after the party? We can talk then."

"I don't want to call you after. I want you to go with me," she said as Jessica pulled away.

"Just call me later, okay?"

"Jess…"

"Have a good time at the party, Venice." Jessica gave her a tight smile and turned to go back inside.

***

The party was in full swing, but Val just wanted to go home. No, that wasn't right. She didn't want to go home; she wanted to go to Jessica.

"Hey, you okay?" Devin asked as she and Jana sat down on the sofa next to her.

"I'm okay."

"You kind of look like someone dragged you here. Did someone drag you here, Val?" she asked.

"No, I came willingly," she said on a sigh.

"Seriously, what's wrong?"

"It's nothing. I'm just in a mood."

"Honey, could you get Val and I something to drink?" Devin asked Jana.

"Sure. Wine? Beer?"

"Just water for me. I'm driving," Val said.

"And a white for you?" Jana asked, kissing Devin on the cheek.

"Yeah, thanks."

Jana left them alone and disappeared into the kitchen.

"Spill," Devin said.

"It's complicated."

"What in life isn't these days?"

"You know how I'm kind of friends with Dani and Peyton?"

"How are you *kind of* friends with people? You're either friends, or you're not."

"I don't hang out with them often."

"I don't hang out often with Barb, but she's still my friend."

"Anyway… You know how I know them?"

"Yes, and Kenzie Smythe, Lennox Owen, and whoever else they hang out with."

"Well, I kind of met someone in that same group. She used to be, anyway. She dated Maddox, who's friends with Dani, Peyton, Kenzie, and Lennox. They broke up, and it ended badly. Jessica came out on the wrong side of the breakup."

"Jessica?"

"Yeah, Jessica. She and I met by coincidence, and she likes me."

"A Jessica who dated a Maddox… Shit, Val. Are you dating Jessica Morrison?!" Devin practically yelled.

"Keep your voice down, Dev." Val placed a hand over her friend's mouth for good measure. Then, she removed it. "You don't just yell something like that."

"Why not? You're dating a woman that's been on the cover of the swimsuit issue more than five times, Val."

Val thought about Jessica in that bikini for a second but then shook herself out of it.

"I don't know what we're doing, exactly."

"If it involves sex, it's probably dating."

"We haven't done that yet."

"Yet? You think it's likely?"

"Not with what happened earlier tonight."

"Tell me," Devin said.

Val filled her in on their first meeting at the shop. She also told her about Dani's gallery opening, and the next day when Val orchestrated another chance to see her.

"She was the one you got the flowers for? I've been so preoccupied with the move, I forgot to ask about that."

"That was her. It was supposed to be a friendship thing."

"But now it's not just friendship?"

Val explained what had happened in the infinity pool, and then earlier tonight at Jessica's house.

"I don't know what's wrong with me." She leaned back against the sofa.

"You always doubt your worth; that's what's wrong with you."

"I don't doubt my worth." Val looked at her.

"Yes, you do. You work at the mailbox store because you don't think you can do any better, but you easily could. You want to buy your own franchise because you think it'll look better if you own your own business – which no one you know actually cares about. Apparently, you think you're not good enough for a woman who seems to really like you, from what you told me. Val, you can't even say you're friends with four famous women. You have to say you're *kind of* friends because you don't think you fit in with them."

"Have you seen them? I don't."

"Sweetie, I do see you." Devin smiled at her. "You're the one that doesn't see how good you are." She looked behind Val and said, "Thanks, babe."

Jana handed her a white wine and Val a bottle of water.

"Thanks, Jana," Val said as Jana sat back down next to Devin.

"Do you want this woman, Val?"

"I think so."

"And does she want you as you are, and not whoever you think you're supposed to be?"

"I think so."

"Then, get out of here and go get her." She patted Val's leg.

"Go get who?" Jana asked.

"Val's got a crush," Devin told her.

"I do not have a crush," Val argued.

"So, you like her a lot?"

"What is this, grade school? Yes, I like her a lot."

"Then, go tell her that." Devin shoved her playfully.

***

"Hello?"

"Jess, it's me. Can I come in?"

"Who's me?"

"Jess, please."

"It's early. How was the party?"

"I'd love to tell you in person instead of into this speaker box."

"You were supposed to call," Jessica said.

"I came here to apologize, Jess."

"You could have done that over the phone."

"I brought Sour Patch Kids," she said, shaking the box in case Jessica could hear it through the speaker.

"You're trying to bribe me with candy?"

"I'm trying to apologize to you and give you candy. There's a difference."

"I don't know, Venice. Maybe you were right," Jessica said, sounding defeated.

"No, I was an idiot. Can I please come in and tell you that to your face?"

"I had a couple glasses of wine; and by a couple, I mean, I finished the bottle."

"So, you're drunk?"

"I'm tipsy."

"And you don't want to see me when you're tipsy?"

"I want to see you all the time, Venice," the woman replied.

"Then, open the gate, babe," Val said.

It took a minute, but the gate opened, and Val drove through it and up the driveway. She parked and got to the door quickly enough to ring the bell once before Jessica opened it.

"Hey," she said, looking a little sad. "Where's my candy?"

Val held the box out for her and said, "Here you go."

"Just one box this time?" Jessica said, taking it from her.

"Did you eat the other two already?"

"Yeah, when you showed up tonight, acted like an

asshole, and left for your party, I ate both of them."

"I am sorry." Val walked into the house when Jessica turned around and started walking to the living room. "I have some self-esteem issues I need to work through."

"I have another bottle of wine I'd planned on working through. Care to join me?"

"Jess, can we just talk without the wine?"

Val sat down next to Jessica on her sofa, looked at the coffee table where she saw the two empty candy boxed, and turned to Jessica.

"I just wanted to go to a party with you, Venice. Is it too much too soon for you, me meeting your friends? I'd introduce you to mine, but I don't really have any, and the ones I used to have, you already know."

"No, it's not too soon. I don't care at all about you meeting my friends, Jess."

"Then, why do you keep acting like I'm better than you?"

"Because, sometimes, that's what it feels like," Val answered honestly.

"Why?" the woman asked, not seeming all that tipsy now.

"I think I've always been this way, honestly. It's not you."

"You're like this with Dani and Peyton, too?"

"Again, I've never made out with Dani or Peyton. I definitely haven't made out with Kenzie or Len, either." Val smiled and reached for Jessica's hand, which she let her take. "Jess, we don't know each other all that well yet, but if we're going to keep doing what we're doing, we need to address that."

"We talked for hours the other night."

"And we should talk for hours and hours more," she replied, entwining their fingers as their hands lay on the sofa between them.

"Then, let's do it," Jessica said.

"What? Now?" Val chuckled.

CHAPTER 15

"YES, now," Jessica told her. "I'm not all that tipsy anymore. I'll grab us some water and put on some coffee, and we'll dig deep down into the esteem issue you seem to have." She stood, letting go of Venice's hand in the process.

"That's not exactly what I meant."

"Well, it's what we're doing," Jessica replied as she walked in the direction of her kitchen. "You came over here. If you would have called, you could have just hung up on me."

"I could still drive away," Venice said.

Jessica turned back to her and softly said, "Don't."

Venice just nodded in response. Jessica grabbed water from her refrigerator before she started the coffee. She had a French press, so it would take a minute. That was a good thing because she needed some time. She took a couple of deep breaths as she grabbed them some snacks as well. Venice was here. She had left her party early and had come back because she needed to apologize. Jessica smiled to herself; that was a good sign. Venice was invested enough not to just walk away.

Jessica was proud of herself, too. In her past, she would have just gone to the party. This time, she stood her ground and asked more from her partner. Well, Venice wasn't her partner. They weren't even technically dating. They'd had one date; singular. Tonight was supposed to be their second. Maybe it still could be. Jessica poured the coffee when it was ready, remembering how Venice took hers, and prepared a tray, which she had found tucked between the cabinets and the fridge. Nice one, Carol. She carried everything out to the living room.

"Oh, wow." Venice stood. "Let me help."

"I've got it," she replied, placing the tray on the table. "Us, femmes, can carry trays, you know?" she teased.

Venice laughed and sat back down.

"Well, us, butches, like to help and sometimes do the physical labor," she replied.

"Do you consider yourself a butch?" Jessica asked her as she sat back down next to her.

"In some ways." Venice shrugged a shoulder.

"What ways?"

"I don't know. I guess I'd describe myself as a mild butch."

"Mild?" Jessica laughed as she took the coffee she'd made for Venice and passed it to her.

"Yeah, I don't know. Like, there are stereotypes and stuff. I think I fit into some of those, but not all of them. I wouldn't describe myself as femme, though. I guess I lean toward butch but would be somewhere along the overall spectrum."

"How do you lean toward it?" Jessica asked, picking up her own cup.

"Well, I did wear a tux," Venice said, smiling at her.

"That you did, babe," Jessica replied, thinking about how good this woman had looked in it. "And, let me just say, you–"

"I know. Everyone was a fan of the tux." Venice laughed.

"Who else told you they were a fan?" Jessica questioned.

"Why? Are you jealous?"

"Was it Paula?"

Venice burst out laughing, placed her cup back on the table, and said, "Come here, please." She patted her lap.

Jessica wasn't sure if she just wanted her to put her feet in her lap or if she wanted Jessica to straddle her. Jessica just put her feet there.

"Was it Paula?" she asked.

"She liked it, yes, but I'm here with you, Jessica. I don't care about Paula in the slightest."

"What about Peyton's dream where you two have two point five kids and a house in the burbs together?"

"I don't think I should have the point five. I'd stop at two," Venice teased. "And that's Peyton's dream. It's not mine."

"What's yours?" Jessica asked, taking a drink of her still way too hot coffee.

"Right now, I don't know."

"You don't know?"

"No. I mean, do you know your dream?"

"Be taken seriously as an actress so I can keep getting good jobs and not crap because I love what I do now; find a woman I'm crazy about who also happens to be crazy about me; marry the crap out of her; and then maybe pop out two point five kids."

"Well, it'll never work between us if you're still stuck on that point five," Venice joked.

"I'm willing to negotiate on either two or three," she replied. Then, she placed her mug on the table and slid a little closer, her thighs now over Venice's lap. "You really don't have a dream like that?" She leaned her elbow on the back of the sofa and stared at the beautiful Venice Valentine.

"I know I want a wife. I'd like to have kids, but I know I don't want to have them myself."

"Mild butch." Jessica coughed as if to cover up her comment.

Venice laughed and said, "Hey, I'd much rather our kids have your genes than mine."

"Why do you say that?" Jessica asked, brushing right past the topic of them having kids together.

"Well, I don't have the best family history, and what you've told me about yours leads me to believe that if there are kids in our future, they'd be better off coming out of you." Venice rubbed her hands over Jessica's thighs.

"Tell me why." Jessica ran her hand through Venice's hair.

"My grandfather died from lung cancer on my mom's side; probably from smoking, but still. My grandmother on my dad's side died after three-too-many heart attacks and the complications that came from them. My other two grandparents both had diabetes."

"Oh, wow," Jessica said.

"And my father was an alcoholic. He's in recovery now and hasn't had a drink in eighteen years, but my mom smoked for about twenty years and only recently quit for good, so there are diseases all over my family tree with a healthy side of addiction."

"You seem to be okay," Jessica replied.

"I am. I'm high risk for stuff, but I go to the doctor. I drink, but I don't go crazy. I've never smoked because it's never interested me. I did have a pretty sizeable baseball card collection, though, so I think I've funneled my addictive family trait into something positive."

"Baseball cards?"

"Yeah, I started collecting them as a kid, and then I just kept going. It wasn't worth all that much. I had a couple of really good cards, though."

"Had?"

"I sold most of them a few years ago."

"Why?"

"My ex-girlfriend, who was my current girlfriend at the time, got into a really bad car accident. The other driver didn't have insurance. She was in the hospital for several weeks and didn't have health insurance at the time."

"You helped pay her expenses?"

"It was either that, or she'd be in debt up to her eyeballs while she was trying to recover. It wasn't a big deal.

I just sold the cards and took care of what I could for her. She's still technically paying me back because she couldn't just take the money. She sends me a check whenever she can. It'll be a hundred bucks here or two hundred there. I didn't cash the first three, and she came knocking on my door complaining, so I just gave in. That's part of what I have saved for my store."

"You are such a good person, Venice." Jessica kissed her cheek and kept her lips hovering there for a minute. "And isn't that your dream?"

"What?"

"Owning the store?"

"It just seemed like the next step."

"Why?" Jessica kissed her cheek again.

"Because I think it would be good to own my own business instead of just working for someone else."

"You've always wanted that?"

"Not specifically a pack and ship place, but I have always wanted something to call my own, I guess. Being my own boss also has a nice ring to it."

"And you think you'll be happy owning something like that?"

"I don't know. I guess I never thought about it in terms of happiness."

"Babe, what?" Jessica pulled back a little to look at her. "You've never thought about your professional goals and how they relate to your happiness?"

"I've never known what I want to do professionally, Jess. I'm not like you. I thought college would help me figure it out, but I settled for philosophy because it seemed easy enough, and I thought it would keep my interest for four years."

"Have you ever thought about going back to school now?"

"At thirty-five?"

"Why not? People do it all the time."

"But, why would I? What would be the point? I did it

already. I've got the dusty diploma stuffed in a box somewhere to prove it."

"But you weren't into it then, Venice." Jessica placed her hand on top of Venice's on her knee. "You chose a major just to choose it and graduate. You're older and wiser now. Maybe there's something else out there that interests you. College could be a nice way to check it out without any real consequences. You could take a class or two just to see. You've got nothing to lose, really."

"My wallet would sure lose something," Venice replied.

"But wouldn't it be worth it?" Jessica smiled at her. "Hey, it's up to you. It was just an idea. If you want that store, I say keep going for it. But if you don't know for sure that you want it, don't feel it in your bones that this is the dream you have for yourself, then stop saving up for it and start searching for what you do want, Venice."

Venice turned her face to her then, gave her a soft smile, and said, "No one's ever said that to me before."

"What?"

"Devin tried to tonight, I guess. She was more concerned with me making things up to you than the business stuff, but no one has ever really encouraged me before."

"I'll encourage you," Jessica replied, cupping Venice's cheek in the process. "However you want; I'll encourage you, babe."

"And you promise me that you don't care about the fact that my degree is useless, my car will likely die soon, my–"

Jessica kissed her softly and pulled back to look into those dark brown eyes.

"That's all stuff, Venice. Stuff changes. I didn't grow up with all of this." She looked around her living room. "And it could all be taken away tomorrow. It's just stuff. I like it, and I'd like it to stick around, but if it left tomorrow, and I had to crash with you in your apartment because I had no money and no stuff, I'd be okay with that. I want a person who wants me back." Jessica shrugged. "And I want a life with that person. Even if I never get cast in another movie again, if I have that person and our life together, I'll be happy. I'll be okay."

"That's really all you care about in the end?" Venice asked her.

"Not just in the end. It's all I care about right now, and it feels kind of like a beginning to me, Venice."

CHAPTER 16

VAL woke up to a snoring head on her chest. As she looked down at Jessica, who had an arm draped around her waist and was still sleeping soundly, she thought to herself that at least Jessica wasn't perfect. She smiled as Jessica snorted and then couldn't hold in her laughter when she snorted again, but louder this time.

"Are you laughing at my snoring?" Jessica asked, waking up, likely because Val was shaking with laughter beneath her.

"Maybe," she replied.

"That's not very nice," Jessica said, running a hand under Val's shirt to rest on her abdomen. "I let you stay over and everything."

"You let me stay over because we were up talking until three in the morning, and you didn't want me driving home so late."

"Well, I have heard such great things about your car," Jessica said sarcastically. "What time is it?" she asked as she lifted her head, her long hair a mess around it.

"About nine," Val replied. "I have to be at work by eleven today. I'm closing. I should probably–"

"If you say you should probably go, I'm going to be very upset with you," Jessica said, rolling off of her and onto her back. "I at least need a hug before you run out on me."

"I can do one better," Val replied, rolling on top of her and looking down into those hazel eyes.

"There you go again, selling yourself short. This is way more than one better."

Jessica wrapped her arms around Val's neck and pulled her down for a kiss, morning breath and all. Val loved kissing this woman. There was just something that washed over her whenever they did this that made her feel safe and wanted at the same time. It didn't hurt that Jessica made little sounds all the time that indicated just how much she wanted Val. Val's hand slid up and under Jessica's shirt and rested just below her breast.

"You should keep going," Jessica encouraged.

"If I start, I won't want to stop," Val replied, kissing Jessica's neck now.

"Who says you have to?"

"I do, Jess." Val kissed her lips. "I have to go to work."

"I hate your job right now," Jessica said, kissing her again.

Val sat back up, straddling her, and said, "Why don't you come over tomorrow night?"

"To your place?"

"Yeah."

Jessica smiled and asked, "Why not tonight?"

"Because I'll be at the store until at least nine. Plus, I need some time to clean it up a little. Devin, the tornado, had left her part of the place a mess."

Jessica's hands slid up the back of Val's shirt and rubbed her back, leaving goosebumps wherever she touched.

"I'll be there. Should I bring anything?"

"Just you," Val said. "We can order in if that's okay. I don't have a lot of food in my fridge. Maybe you can bring over a copy of that new movie you're in. There's got to be some benefit to dating a movie star, right?" She winked at her.

"Oh, there is," Jessica replied, sitting up and lifting Val's shirt a little as she did. "But it has nothing to do with advanced copies of my movie, sexy." She kissed Val's stomach. "And I don't like watching myself anyway."

"Why not?"

"I think my voice sounds weird on camera, and I keep thinking I could have done a better job if I'd only had another take."

Val held Jessica's face in her hands and said, "Well, then we'll watch something else." She quickly climbed out of bed. "I'm going to pee, and then I'll head out."

"You even make that sound sexy." Jessica flopped back on the bed and placed a hand over her eyes.

"You okay?"

"I think I'm slightly hungover."

"Aspirin?"

"That would be amazing."

"Medicine cabinet?"

"Yeah. And I think I have the stuff for Carol's hangover cure smoothie. I'll make that after you go."

Venice returned from the attached master bathroom to the bedroom with a glass of water and a few aspirin tablets.

"Take these. Stay in here. I'll make it for you before I go."

"I thought you had to run."

"I do, but I can do this first." Val kissed her, leaning down over Jessica for an extra moment. "I'll bring it back in here. Just rest, okay?"

"Okay," the woman replied.

Val made her way into the kitchen after Jessica told her where the recipe was located. She pulled it out of the drawer first, read it over a couple of times, found the blender and the ingredients, and started mixing everything together.

"Hello?" a voice came from behind her.

Val turned around to see a strange woman standing there.

"Hello."

"Where's Jess?" she asked.

"Depends on who's asking."

"I'm Carol, her assistant."

"Oh, hi." Val smiled. "I'm Val." She moved the few steps forward and held out her hand. "It's nice to meet you."

Carol gave her an expression she couldn't read and asked, "Where is she?"

"She's in her room." Val nodded proudly that she'd been able to answer the question for some reason.

"And you stayed over?"

Val stopped the blender and said, "I don't know what she'd want me to tell you."

"You can tell her everything," Jessica said as she emerged, looking adorable in a pair of light-pink sleep shorts and a white tank top with no bra on under it. "I already do." She gave Carol a hug. "Happy to have you back."

"Are you? Seems like I've been replaced," she replied, hooking a thumb back at Val.

"Val is not my assistant." Jessica looked over at her. "If she were, I'd be in trouble for sexual harassment." She wiggled her eyebrows at Val and walked over to her. "Sorry, I forgot she'd be back this morning." She kissed Val's lips. "And, thank you for this." She nodded toward the blender.

"You're welcome," Val replied as Jessica's hands went to her neck, and her thumbs stroked her skin. "Should I go?"

"You could call in sick and stay for as long as you want. I'm not kicking you out," Jessica replied, smiling at her. "Carol might, though, if you keep trying to take over her job."

"It's true," Carol joked from behind them.

"I should get going." Val kissed Jessica quickly. "I hope I made it right, but I doubt it's as good as yours," she said to Carol.

"Oh, I like her. Keep her, Jess."

"I'm trying to," Jessica said softly as her lips brushed Val's once more.

***

Val had a decent day at the office, as they say. She had only one pretty angry customer, which was better than other days when she had at least two. Somehow, it was her fault that the rates for overnight shipping were so high or that the package that had to get there by tomorrow would have to disrupt the space-time continuum to do so. She always just took it and tried to keep things civil as she processed the shipments. She had an afternoon visit from the boss, Louis Hedlund. He owned sixteen franchises and hardly made an appearance even once a month. She doubted that he was as well-off as he liked to pretend he was, but he had chosen great locations for his stores, and he'd made a lot of money while not doing much of the daily work himself.

He'd asked her some questions about why Nick had had four hours of overtime this month, and Shawna had had six. Two of the other employees had had four hours each as well. Louis had suggested they hire another full-time employee so that he wouldn't have to pay overtime. She'd mentioned that they had only worked eighteen hours of overtime in total. So, a forty-hour a week employee would be overkill. She suggested adjusting the schedule a bit first, and if that didn't help, she could hire a part-timer instead. He had left after reviewing some paperwork, and she and Nick took care of the after-business hours rush together before he clocked out and went home.

Val sat in the back-office area alone for a while longer than she normally did. She had finished the end of the night paperwork and readied the bank deposit that she'd toss in the night drop box on her walk to her car. She normally tried to get out of here as soon as she could at the end of the night, especially after she closed.

"That should tell me something," she said to herself,

staring at the spreadsheet on the computer screen in front of her.

The only thing she'd ever thought about doing was running a business for herself. It never mattered what that business was. Her father had been a failed business owner, trying his hands at landscaping with no earthly idea what he was doing. Because he had been drinking back then, he'd lost a finger using a weed whacker and nearly lost his whole hand in the process. They'd been able to reattach the digit, but it never worked the same again. That only caused him to drink more, and eventually, he lost the company.

Her mother, too, had been a failed entrepreneur. She'd gone to cosmetology school after having Val, trying to find a way to make some extra money. She had done so for a bit as a part of a salon inside a department store, but when she opted to go out on her own, thinking she'd make more money, it didn't last. She went back to another department store salon after about two years of trying to make it work. Neither of her parents had really ever been unemployed. They had just both bounced back into other jobs, but for whatever reason, Val had always hung on to the idea that she could do it. She could run her own business. She could be effective as an owner and as a manager of employees and make money at the same time to support herself and her family.

She just had no idea what kind of business she wanted to run. The shipping place had been an obvious choice. She had already worked her way up to the top of one store. She could easily run the day to day in one she owned until she decided to expand and hire someone else to manage it, like Louis had with her and his other managers. She hadn't taken any business classes in college the first time around. Maybe that was what she should do now. She could take something at a community school, see if it was for her or not, and it wouldn't cost an arm and a leg. If she liked it enough, she could decide what to do then.

She tabbed over to the browser and searched for

community colleges in the area before she clicked on the top result and then on the course catalog page. Several clicks later, she had reviewed the summaries for many of the business classes on offer and had narrowed it down to three for herself. The fall semester wouldn't start for several months, but there were two six-week summer sessions. She didn't register. She just saved a few of the links for herself to review later on her own laptop. After emailing them to herself, she checked the time. It was well after ten. She probably shouldn't call Jessica. The woman was likely already asleep. They'd been up all night talking. Val felt like she was about to drop herself, but she didn't want to fall asleep tonight without talking to Jessica again.

She locked the store, walked around the corner to the bank, dropped the deposit, and made it to her car. She drove the short distance to her apartment, found street parking not all that far away, and after locking the front door behind her, she immediately reached for her phone. She hoped she hadn't missed her chance. She walked into her bedroom as the phone rang.

"Hey," Jessica said, sounding sleepy.

"Did I wake you?"

"No, I was just reading a script in bed. I was thinking about calling it a night, though. Someone kept me up until three in the morning last night."

"She sounds like a bitch," Val joked.

"She was. She kept me up talking. I didn't even get to second base."

Val laughed and said, "I just wanted to call to say goodnight."

There was a silence between them before Jessica said, "Are you in bed?"

"Not yet. I just got home."

"Long day?"

"You could say that." Val sighed.

"Why don't you get ready for sleep? I'll hang on the line. Then, we can say goodnight."

"You sound tired."

"You kept me up until three in the morning," Jessica replied, laughing.

"I just mean that you should go to sleep. I still have to brush my teeth and–"

"Venice, brush your teeth and that sexy, wavy hair you have, and then FaceTime me."

"FaceTime?"

"I want to see you."

"Okay. Ten minutes?"

"I'll be here."

And she was there ten minutes later, when Val called her back, and they saw each other as they exchanged their goodnights.

CHAPTER 17

"I THOUGHT it would be a long time before I saw you again," Lisa said as Jessica entered her LA workspace.

It was a giant loft in an old warehouse with cracked windows and graffiti on one wall. There were art tables on either side of the main aisle and racks and racks of clothes all around. Yards of fabric were on the tables, the floor, and leaning against the walls. It was just as Lisa had always dreamed; she'd once told Jessica all about it in one of their friend moments before they'd begun the benefits part of their relationship.

"Is now still a good time?"

"It's fine. I have models coming in soon, unless you want to take some test shots in my new line for me." Lisa smirked at her.

"No, I'm retired."

"Since when?"

"I think I just decided recently."

"Because of acting?" Lisa asked.

"I'm not exactly the fresh-faced model I once was. I mean, I don't have my own reality show or a million followers on Instagram. That seems to be what people want in a model these days."

"Well, you still have the face and the body for it if you ask me," Lisa replied as she walked behind a rack of clothes. "Let's go into my office to talk."

"Your office is just behind a screen. Can we go for a coffee or somewhere without your employees?"

"I can't leave right now, Jess." The woman reappeared, pushing the rack of clothes toward another woman who took it and continued on. "We can go outside, though. There's a back staircase where the models usually smoke."

"Okay."

They made their way through the double doors and outside to the staircase that was next to the giant garage doors where trucks could pull in and load up.

"So, I told you I'd ship your stuff, but I found out when I got home that I don't have any of your stuff to ship. Did I miss something? Is that why you called?" Lisa asked her.

"No, that's not why," Jessica replied.

Lisa sat down on the second stair from the bottom. Jessica joined her but left space between them.

"Care to tell me what's going on, then? I know you're not here to get back together. And before you say anything – I know we weren't really together. You don't need to tell me."

"I came to apologize."

"You already did that," Lisa replied.

"I need to do it again."

"Why?"

"Because I never should have–"

"Don't start with that again, okay?" Lisa turned toward her, leaning against the rusty staircase railing. "Jess, we were friends before we had sex. You talked to me about Maddox and how she wasn't treating you right. I talked to you about things, too. I knew what I was doing, though. You had a girlfriend. You never hid that from me. And I knew when I started flirting with you that I wanted more. And I didn't just want more; I wanted you. I wanted to take you from her and make you mine. That didn't exactly work out. I should have known that the first time when you ended things with me to give things with Maddox another chance. It's fine. You don't have to apologize again. I was a big girl every time we hooked up. It was my decision."

"Did I lead you on? If I did, I–"

"Jess, I don't know what's going on with you, but we're good." Lisa leaned forward and shrugged. "I like you. I wish you felt the same way, but we were good for what we were: two women who liked having sex with each other."

"We were friends, though, like you said."

"We were, yeah."

"Not anymore?" Jessica asked.

"Not now, at least." The woman moved to stand. "I don't need another apology, and I'll get over it in time, but I wanted a girlfriend, Jessica. I need to get over how I feel about you before we can go back to being friends."

"Okay. I understand," Jessica replied, standing, too.

"I have to get back inside. The models will be here soon," Lisa said.

"Good luck. Your line looks great from what I could see."

"Thanks. I'll see you around, okay?"

"Sure."

She hadn't known what to expect when she'd called Lisa and asked to meet, but this was probably the best outcome. Lisa had been clear throughout their friendship that she wanted more than that. Jessica had been clear, too, though, that she hadn't. They were adults, and they made decisions that led them here. At least Jessica felt like they could be friends one day, assuming she didn't do anything else stupid to Lisa in the future.

It was time for another possibly awkward visit on her apology world tour. When she entered the office, she noticed how clean and white it was – the opposite of the old warehouse she had just visited.

"I'm here to see Avery Simpson."

"May I–" the receptionist said as she looked up. "Oh, hi."

"Hi," Jessica said, realizing she'd been recognized. "I have an appointment, I think. Well, I called, and she said it was fine if I stopped by."

"Right. She's in her office. It's just through there." The receptionist pointed down the wide hallway. "Turn left at the elevator. You can't miss it."

"Thanks," Jessica replied with a smile.

She walked down the hall of the tech start-up. Well, was an app company considered a start-up? She didn't know. It looked like a start-up from the dry-erase board walls and ping-pong table off to the side with two rather nerdy-looking guys playing a game. She turned left and found Avery sitting behind a desk in an office made entirely of glass. Seriously, it was four walls of glass, and Jessica could see desks and computers behind it, meaning this place was bigger than she had originally thought.

"Hey, come in," Avery said when Jessica knocked on the door. "Sorry, I would have met you out there. I just got stuck in my own brain."

"No, it's fine. I got a chance to see your office a little. It's nice."

"Thanks. We just expanded again. It's pretty crazy. I never thought I'd be running a company. I just wanted to make an app that would help people sleep."

"I haven't used it myself, but I did check it out in the app store. It has great reviews."

"Have a seat," Avery said, giving Jessica the open palm gesture toward one of the chairs in front of her desk. "And, yeah, it's doing well." She paused. "So, what can I do for you?"

"Have you talked to Kenz or Len?"

"Recently, no. I think Maddox has, though. Why?"

"I don't know if I'm doing the right thing or not, but I feel like I should, so I'm just going to do it, okay?"

"Okay…" Avery looked concerned now.

"I'm sorry for how I acted at the party."

"Dani's thing?" Avery asked.

"No, the New Year's Eve party when Lisa and I kind of–"

"Oh, that party." Avery leaned forward in her chair.

"You're apologizing to me?"

"Yeah, I feel like I should. I was in a bad place that night. The relationship I'd had after Maddie had ended. I was on-again, off-again with Lisa, and Maddie wasn't up for talking to me that night because she was trying to find you." She smiled at Avery. "And I wanted to tell her how I felt without caring about how she felt at the time."

"For what it's worth, Maddox is in a good place now."

"I know. I'm working my way up to her." Jessica chuckled. "I just wanted to tell you that I'm sorry Lisa and I burst in on the two of you, and for how I acted when I saw you two together in bed."

"You know we were just talking, right?"

"I do, but even if you weren't, I had no right to treat you or Maddie that way. She's a free woman. She has… No, she was a free woman. She's now a taken woman."

Avery chuckled and said, "I don't know about the word 'taken,' but Maddox is my love, and I'm very lucky to have her."

"She's lucky to have you, too, though. Trust me, I don't see Maddie a lot these days, but I still stalk social media to make sure she and I aren't going to run into one another all the time, and I can see how happy she is with you, Avery."

"Thank you for saying that. I don't imagine it's easy to say something like that to your ex-girlfriend's current girlfriend."

"It's easier now than it would have been a few years ago," Jessica said.

"What about you?"

"What about me?"

"Love? Anyone special?"

She smiled and said, "Yeah, there's someone pretty special."

"Really? Who's the lucky lady?"

"You actually think a woman who'd date me would be lucky?"

"Jess, I wasn't around when all the craziness happened between you and Maddox. I know it hurt her, and that makes me sad because I don't want anything or anyone to ever hurt the woman I love, but you made a mistake. No one is perfect. We're all human beings just trying to figure things out every single day. Do I think you and Maddox belonged together? No, but I'm also kind of biased." Avery smiled at her. "I do think there's someone out there for you, though, and that when you find her, assuming you haven't already, you won't make the same mistakes you made before."

"I won't," Jessica stated firmly. "I won't. I shouldn't have before, but I won't again."

"So, who is she?" Avery asked, rubbing her hands together. "Do we know her?"

Jessica didn't know how to answer that question because she and Venice hadn't talked about what this was or what they would tell people.

"I kind of want to keep it to myself right now. Is that okay?"

"Of course," Avery replied.

"Thanks. And thanks for meeting me. I didn't mean to interrupt your day. It's just been important to me lately to try to put the past behind me."

"You're moving on. That's great, Jess."

"I think so," she replied.

***

"I brought myself, as requested," Jessica said as Venice opened the door to her apartment.

"I'm glad. I missed you," the woman replied, tugging on Jessica's hand until she had her inside the apartment.

"You seem happy," Jessica said.

"I am. You're here," Venice told her, kissing Jessica quickly.

"You're sweet." Jessica smiled at her.

"You're beautiful," Venice told her, sliding her fingertips over Jessica's cheek.

"Are you going to give me a tour or just stand there staring at me?"

"If I have a choice, I'll stand here and—"

"Not a choice." Jessica placed her hand over Venice's mouth. "Give me the tour, babe. I want to see your place."

"This is pretty much it," Venice replied, turning around and waving her hand in the air. "Living room and kitchen kind of all-in-one. The bathroom is over there." She pointed down a skinny hallway to the right of the living room. "And the bedrooms are back there, too."

"I assume one of those bedrooms is empty since Devin is gone, but that the other one belongs to you." Jessica wrapped her arms loosely around Venice's neck. "Can I see it?"

"Devin's room? Sure. There's nothing in it anymore."

"Asshole," Jessica replied, playfully shoving Venice's shoulders.

"Come on," the woman said, laughing and pulling on Jessica's hand.

They went down the hall, walking past the old but comfortable-looking sofa, a nice-looking coffee table made of light-colored wood, and a TV stand with a modest-sized flat-screen resting atop it. The bathroom door was closed, so she couldn't see what it looked like, but Venice opened the bedroom door beyond it, and motioned for her to go inside.

"This is your room?"

"Yup. This is it. It's pretty standard as far as rooms go. All the furniture was either bought second-hand or put together by me after a trip to IKEA."

"It's nice. You know, I actually have some IKEA furniture." Jessica turned back to Venice, who followed her into the room.

"You do not."

"You doubt me?"

"I do," she said.

"I have a fine Ingatorp table in one of my guest rooms. It has a bay window. I wanted a small round table. My interior designer actually found it for me. So, there." She crossed her arms over her chest.

"You remember the name of the table?" Venice asked as she laughed.

"I do. It sounded funny, so I remembered it."

"Well, I have been appropriately scolded." Venice held up both of her hands in defense. "Consider me lectured."

"I consider you sexy," Jessica replied.

Venice lowered her hands and looked behind Jessica toward the bed, which was a queen with no duvet but a thin tan blanket and some plain white sheets under it. It suited her somehow.

"What do you want to order for dinner?" Venice asked.

"Are you an option?"

"Really? That joke is a little dated, babe," Venice said.

"No, I'm bringing it back," Jessica replied.

"No, you're really not. And because you made it, I get to pick dinner and the movie."

"That's not fair," Jessica said as she was pulled back into the hallway.

"I have Sour Patch Kids in the kitchen."

"Okay. You can pick dinner and the movie," Jessica replied.

CHAPTER 18

"YOU really don't like them?" Jessica asked her.

"Nope."

"Good. More for me."

"They're all for you. That's why I bought them," Val told her, passing the yellow box back over to Jessica.

"So, we've had dinner, and we've watched the movie," Jessica said rather slowly.

"We did, yes," Val replied, running her hands along Jessica's legs, which were in her lap.

They were on the sofa. Val was sitting up on one side, and Jessica was lying down, eating Sour Patch Kids for dessert.

"What do you want to do now?"

"Well, we could watch another movie," Val suggested. "It's only ten."

"We could," Jessica replied, folding the two parts of the lid over one another and placing the candy on the coffee table. "We've stayed up way later than that before."

"True."

"What else could we do, though?" Jessica asked, sitting up and sliding her legs under her body, facing Val.

"We could go out if you want. I'm not working tomorrow. Did you want to go to that bar, Wonderland?"

"We could." Jessica moved a little closer and then straddled Val's hips. "What else could we do, though? Any other options?"

"No, I can't think of anything," Val said, running her hands up and down Jessica's sides, smiling up at her.

"Really? Nothing? That's disappointing."

"Jess…"

"Yes?" Jessica's lips hovered above her own, dangerously close.

"I want to."

"Then, let's."

"I'm going to hate myself for saying this, but I don't think we should."

"You just told me you have tomorrow off." Jessica's hips rocked into her, causing Val to close her eyes at the sensation. "And I know you want to."

"Oh, I do. You have no idea."

"Yes, I do, because I feel it too, babe." Jessica rolled them again.

"Jessica, hold on, okay?"

"I'm holding, babe, but I want this. I want you. I want us to be together." She rolled them a third time. "Tell me why you want to keep waiting."

"Because I need to talk to Maddox," she blurted out.

"What?" Jessica's hips stopped. She then pulled back a little and gave Val a hard-to-read expression. "You need to talk to my ex-girlfriend?"

"She's my friend, Jess, and you're her ex."

"So, this is like a bro-code thing?" she asked, hopping off Val's body and sitting beside her instead.

"It's not like that, exactly, but I do think I should tell her what we're doing."

"What are we doing?" Jessica asked.

"Jess, don't pull away, okay?" she asked quickly when Jessica turned her body toward the TV and swung her long legs over the sofa, pressing her feet to the floor and leaning her body forward.

"I'm not pulling away, Venice. I just want to know. We haven't talked about what we're doing. Well, we did, and you brought up the reasons not to, but we clearly still are, so I guess I just want to know if this is going to continue, or if you'll come up with another reason why it shouldn't."

"Hey," Val began softly, placing a hand under Jessica's shirt on her lower back. "I'm not sitting around coming up with reasons why we shouldn't do this, Jess. I had two."

"Had?"

"I'm still working on the whole self-esteem thing. It about killed me to show you my spartan bedroom in there, but I still did it. I'm a work in progress."

"And the other reason?"

"That I wasn't sure you were ready?"

"Yeah, that one."

"I don't know. You tell me."

"And if I do, you'll trust me?" Jessica asked. "You'll trust my answer?"

"Yes, I will. Jess, I trust you. I hope you know that. I'm not thinking about all the ways this can go wrong. I'm trying to focus on how good it feels because it's going right."

Jessica sighed and leaned back, causing Val to remove her hand and turn to face the woman, emulating Jessica's sitting position from moments ago.

"I've been making the rounds."

"Rounds?"

"I started with Dani at the show. I apologized to her for how I hurt Maddie and my friendship with her and everyone else."

"You did?"

"And then, I talked to Kenzie and Len."

"You talked to Lennox?"

"She's a softie whenever her wife is around. Make a note of that in case you ever need to apologize to her for something."

"How'd it go?"

"I realized I missed my friends," Jessica replied.

"You lost all of them, didn't you?"

"I used to feel guilty, but it was because of what I'd lost. Now, I feel the loss and guilt separately. Like, I know what I did was wrong, and I feel terrible because I did it and for the pain I caused, but I also just miss my friends."

"Did you tell them that?"

"Kind of. It was short. They had Liam with them, so they couldn't stay long, but I want a Liam, Venice."

"You want Liam?" Val checked.

"No, I want *a* Liam. I want my own baby one day, and I know it takes a village. They have a village, Venice. They have each other, and their kids will grow up surrounded by that kind of love. I want that for my kids, and I want my friends back."

"Did they accept your apology?"

"They did. I think it'll take some time, but Kenzie was more open to it than Lennox was. I think I could offer to babysit Liam, and Kenzie would take me up on it while Lennox glares at me for a few minutes and then says yes."

"That sounds like them," Val replied, chuckling at the characterization of her friends.

"I talked to Avery, too, and Lisa, but she said we were fine."

"You talked to Lisa?" Val asked, swallowing hard and wishing her voice hadn't gone up an octave when she'd asked the question.

Jessica turned her face to her, lifted an eyebrow, and gave her a smirk.

"Jealousy?"

"Yup," Val answered honestly. "Rearing its ugly head."

"We talked for all of five minutes," Jessica said. "Nothing to be jealous about."

"And Avery?"

"Definitely nothing to be jealous about with Avery. She's into Maddie," Jessica teased.

"Be serious." Val laughed as she shoved lightly at her shoulder.

"She's okay. She said we're okay, too. I told her I wanted to talk to Maddie next."

"That's a big deal."

"Not as big as Peyton."

"You're talking to Maddox, the one you hurt the most, before you talk to Peyton?"

"I'm sorry. Have you met Peyton Gloss? She's one of the most intense people in the known universe, and she hates me."

"She is, but she doesn't hate you."

"Didn't you tell me she called me Jessica Fucking Morrison, as if that word was my middle name?"

"She did." Val nodded.

"She hates me. Anyway, Maddie's up next." Jessica took a deep breath. "I should be the one to tell her about us."

"Is there an *us*?"

"I hope so. Because if I go into that awkward conversation and tell her about us, and there's no *us*, I'm going to be pretty pissed, Venice."

"You don't think I should be the one to talk to her?"

"Maybe. I don't know. I've never done this before." Jessica sighed again. "I was worried before about talking to her, but now, I'm worried about asking for her forgiveness and then, in that same conversation, telling her that I've been seeing her friend behind her back."

"I'm closer to Avery, if that helps."

Jessica smiled at her and said, "It doesn't, but thank you for trying." Then, she placed a hand on Val's knee. "So, we're not having sex tonight, are we?"

"I don't think so," Val replied. She moved a little closer. "When we do, I don't want to be worrying about Maddox and how she'd take the news of us being together."

"I don't want you thinking about Maddox at all," Jessica said.

"That goes for you, too," Val replied.

Jessica's face softened. She turned her entire body toward Val and gave her shoulders a shove until Val took the hint and laid down. Jessica moved on top of her, stared down at her, and kissed the very tip of her nose.

"I am ready for you, Venice Valentine." She kissed her lips. "I don't want Maddox, Lisa, or anyone else, okay? This is new, but it's right between us. What we're building is worth it. I won't ruin it by lying to you and telling you I'm ready when I'm not."

Val wrapped her arms around her waist and said, "Okay. I trust you."

"So, does that take care of your two reasons?" Jessica asked.

Val smiled up at her and said, "Yeah, it does."

"Good. Then, there is definitely an *us* now."

CHAPTER 19

"AVERY told me you'd be stopping by," Maddox said. "Come on in." She motioned for Jessica to join her in the house.

"Is she here?"

"No, she's hanging out with her brother. He's in town for a few days, and then he's going back on tour."

"He's a performer?"

"No, he does makeup. That's why Avery was at the party where we met. He worked with Peyton. Drink?" she asked, transitioning from one topic to another so quickly, Jessica wasn't prepared.

"What?"

"Do you want a drink, Jess?"

"Water?"

"Sure."

"I like your place." Jessica looked around the modest-sized house with a living room and dining room combo that was smaller than her living room alone. "It's right for you, isn't it?"

"Yeah, it is. It fits for the two of us," the woman replied. "Have a seat. I'll be right there."

Maddox disappeared for a minute, came back with two bottles of water, and asked, "Do you want the tour?"

"Maybe later," Jessica said, wanting to get to the point.

Maddox sat down on the other end of the sofa and passed her the water. Jessica nodded her thanks but didn't open it. She placed it on the table and ran her hands nervously over her jean-clad thighs.

"Out with it, Jess," Maddox said after a long minute of awkward silence.

"You know why I'm here."

"I do. Avery told me."

"I guess that's what happens when you have to apologize to people who are dating."

"Jess, we're beyond this, aren't we?" Maddox asked.

"Beyond what?"

"I don't know; this awkwardness. You're rubbing your jeans so hard, you're going to make holes."

"Oh," she replied and stopped. "I don't know where to start."

"Start at the beginning." Maddox opened her water and took a drink.

"Are you ready to hear it all?" she asked.

"I have no idea, honestly."

"Will you warn me if it's too much? Because I'm kind of hoping to take two steps forward, not one back?"

"I'll do my best, Jess."

Jessica looked out the window next to the sofa at the backyard, where she noticed a swing set.

"Yours?"

"It was here when we moved in." Maddox had followed her eyeline.

"You're going to marry her, aren't you?"

"I hope so," Maddox replied.

"I'm happy for you, Maddie." Jessica smiled genuinely. "So happy."

"I know."

"Do you?"

"Yeah, I do. Jess, I don't hate you anymore. I'm not sure I ever did, but if I did, I don't anymore, okay?"

"When we met, I thought you were it for me," Jessica said.

"I know. I thought the same thing. I remember telling Lennox and Kenzie how happy I was when they met. I used us as a good example."

"Oh, wow."

"I know." Maddox laughed.

"So, what I'm going to say is going to make it sound like I still blame you, but I don't, okay?"

"Just get it all out, Jess. That's what this is, right?"

"Yeah." She swallowed, finding her throat dry, and reached for the water, which she opened and took a drink of before she capped it again. "When we both started traveling like crazy, the honeymoon period was gone just like that." Jessica snapped her fingers. "The problem was, I was still in it. I still wanted to be around you all the time. I wanted to wake up next to you every morning, make love all day, and fall asleep next to each other at night. I don't think I was ready for your career to take off as much as it did so soon after we started dating. I'm glad it did. You're an amazing photographer. But I think I needed someone who needed me in the same way you need your art, Maddie."

"And you felt like I didn't love you as much as I did photography?"

"I felt like I was competing with your job, and I didn't like it. Every time I tried to tell you, there was always a reason why you had to take the next shoot in Egypt or Croatia at the same time we were supposed to spend time together."

"It was work, Jess."

"I know that. I'm not faulting you for it now. I did back then, but I also didn't know how to tell you everything I was feeling."

"Did you really think I didn't love you enough?" the woman asked genuinely.

"That's how it felt sometimes." Jessica shrugged a shoulder. "By the time I realized how bad it had gotten, I'd met Lisa."

"Ah, Lisa. This is my least favorite part of our story."

"I know, but I have to talk about it."

"Just no details, okay? I got enough of an idea when

you walked in on Avery and me."

"I apologized to her for that, but I'm sorry to you, too. I was an asshole."

"I wasn't much better. I lashed out. I could have just talked to you. You're allowed to sleep with Lisa; you're single. And she's single, as far as I know."

"Yeah…" Jessica said, wanting to come back to the topic of her being single a little later.

"So, Lisa and I were friends first, and I talked about you a lot with her."

"Talked about or complained about?"

"Probably mostly complained about, if I'm being honest."

"I figured." Maddox took another drink.

"Anyway, she was so kind to me. She listened, Maddie. That's all it was at first. She'd listen and try to give me advice. I took some of it and left some of it, but it helped, having someone to talk to about how I was feeling."

"It was that bad?" Maddox's expression turned concerned.

"Maddie, we went five weeks without seeing each other, and our goodnight calls went from every night to every so often, and you didn't seem to notice. It made me feel like you didn't care."

"I got so busy. I was trying to find a way to balance it all."

"I know. I just needed more than you could give, Maddie. I don't think that's your fault or mine. It just means we weren't as right for each other as we thought." Jessica looked down at the bottle, still in her hands. "It hurt a lot back then, though. I was still sure you were the one for me, but then there was Lisa, and she was acting like maybe she thought she was. Our friendship grew into something that was inappropriate even before we had sex. She told me how she felt, and I didn't turn her away. I should have turned her away. I knew I didn't want her how I used to want you. But you weren't there, and she was, and it was like I couldn't stop myself from needing to feel wanted by someone else the way she seemed to want me."

"And I wasn't giving that to you," Maddox said softly.

"No matter what was wrong with us, Maddie, what happened next was my fault, and I will always be sorry. If you and I were going to end, it didn't have to end the way that it did."

"I agree with that." Maddox let out a short laugh.

"When it all started with her, I couldn't believe I'd let it." Jessica looked up at the woman. "I felt dirty and guilty and shameful. I showered over and over again after that first time. I cried so loudly in the hotel room where I was staying at the time, I thought the other guests would hear."

"But you still did it again?"

"Because the need that I had overtook the pain after," she replied honestly. "That's all I can really say about it."

"And when it ended?"

"It ended because I loved you, and I knew that if it had a chance of working, I had to stop what I was doing with her, go all-in with you, and see if it was meant to be."

"And then we broke up."

"I think that was the right outcome, but the wrong way to go about it."

"I agree with that, too." Maddox nodded again.

"When I begged for you to take me back, I think it was more because I felt like I needed to make it up to you; like I'd failed you so horribly, and I'd hurt you so badly, that I needed to show you that we could make it work, and that I wanted it to."

"But, you didn't?"

"I did. That's what's so weird. I did. I wanted to make it work. It was just for the wrong reasons. Then, I kissed that girl that meant nothing to me, and that was when it clicked that I didn't want it to work anymore. It was never going to work. It wasn't meant to."

"And then you dated–"

"She was a rebound. It didn't last. If I'm being totally

honest, I didn't cheat on her, but I also wasn't in it all the way, like I was with you."

"And Lisa?"

"You know about Lisa. It's been sex with a side of friendship, at best, with us. But that's been over for a while now."

"She joined your movie, Jess."

"I know, but I didn't tell her to. She just signed onto the project, and I had to deal with it."

"Did you two sleep together?"

"Yes."

"How many times?"

"Three."

"Since then?"

"None." Jessica shook her head. "It's done with Lisa, Maddox."

"You called me Maddox." The woman paused. "You never call me Maddox."

"I've called you Maddie since we met, but I think I should start calling you Maddox like everyone else now."

"Why?"

"Because I want this to be the start of our new relationship; whatever you'll allow that to be."

Maddox took a deep breath and said, "Well, you already managed to convince my girlfriend that you're genuine in your apology and that you want to move on."

"I am, and I do."

"I'm sorry for my part in it, Jessica."

"You usually call me Jess." She gave Maddox a small smile.

"New beginnings," she replied.

"You don't have to apologize, Maddox."

"If you're apologizing for your part, I can own up to mine."

"Fair enough."

"Jessica, you don't carry all the burden for our breakup. You own your actions – whatever they were, but I have to own mine, too. I've talked about what happened a lot with Avery, and she's helped me see that I wasn't blameless. I should have been there for you. I shouldn't have been working so hard; whether it was important for my career or not. Love is the most important thing there is. Finding that person that makes you want to make sacrifices and compromises – and, God – just makes you so very happy, is the best thing in the world."

Jessica smiled and said, "I agree with that."

"So, if you're sorry, and I'm sorry… Does that mean we can, I don't know, be friends one day?" Maddox asked.

"I thought I'd be asking you that question." Jessica laughed softly.

"I'm in if you are."

The weight of the world lifted off of Jessica's shoulders, and she breathed again.

"I'm in," she replied.

Maddox smiled and gave her a hard nod.

"Good."

"Oh, shit," Jessica let out.

"What?"

"I have something else to tell you that might make you change your mind, but I really hope it doesn't."

"Okay…"

"I'm seeing someone. It's new. We haven't even…" Jessica bit her lower lip and held on to it for an extra second to stall. "Anyway, I'm kind of crazy about her."

"I'm happy for you, Jessica."

"You know her," Jessica said, her heart thumping inside her chest.

"I do? Who is it?"

"Venice."

"Val?" Maddox asked a little louder than she'd likely intended.

"I like her first name, but yeah, Val."

"You two are together? Wait. Since when?"

"Since recently. It happened by coincidence at first.

Well, I don't know about that now. It kind of seems like fate, but I had a package that got sent to her store one day. I went to pick it up, and we met. Then, we had this impromptu lunch, and I liked talking to her. I invited her out that night, but I was unclear about my intentions, so she didn't come."

"Really? I can't believe it. You're–"

"We've been talking a lot, Maddox. We've done more talking than anything else. She's being very noble."

"Noble?"

"She wanted to talk to you before we go any further."

"Me?"

"It's a bro-code thing." She took a drink of her water.

"So, Val – who once hit on my current girlfriend – is now dating my ex-girlfriend?"

"That's correct. Like I said, though, she wanted to talk to you before we went any further. If you're mad, please be mad at me and not at her. She's trying to do the right thing. Trust me, we've been close a couple of times to… you know. And she said she wouldn't do anything until she talked to you, but I told her it should be me."

Maddox didn't say anything for a minute. She just stared at a spot on the wall behind Jessica's head.

"I love Val. She's great. She's been such a good friend to Avery, and to me. I think she feels like she's not part of our group, but she is. We all keep trying to tell her, to make her feel like she fits in, but I think it's hard for her."

"It is. She's working on it. I'm trying to help."

"And you really like her?"

"Yes, I do," Jessica said with a smile.

"I can see it; you two. I can see it."

"You can?" Jessica asked, a little surprised.

"Yeah." Maddox nodded. "Just, I don't know, take care of her. Take care of each other."

"So, this is your seal of approval?"

As the front door of the house opened, Maddox laughed and said, "I'm not in charge of who you date; Val, either. I want you both to be happy, so if she makes you happy, and you make her happy, then it's good for me, Jessica."

"Sorry. I'll just disappear while you two talk," Avery said as she walked into the living room.

"No, it's okay. Sit with us," Maddox replied, taking Avery's hand as Avery moved to sit between them on the sofa. "Does she know?" Maddox nodded toward her girlfriend.

"Not who it is." Jessica shook her head.

"Who what is?" Avery asked.

"Jessica's new girl," Maddox replied.

"You told Maddox and not me?" Avery asked, turning toward Jessica.

"It's Val, okay?"

"You're dating Val?" Avery asked, reached for her phone, and then added, "And she didn't tell me? You're both in trouble."

Jessica laughed. Maddox rubbed Avery's back over her shirt as the woman leaned forward, likely to text Venice that she was in trouble. Jessica met Maddox's eyes over Avery. They both smiled. Then, they both nodded.

"We're having a party here. You should come," Maddox told her.

"Yeah?"

"Bring Val."

"I'll ask her."

"Val?" Avery said into her phone. "Yeah, hey. Listen, I'm sitting here with the girlfriend I didn't know you had. Care to explain that?"

Jessica laughed again.

CHAPTER 20

"BUT you have a degree," Val's mom told her.

"I do, but I'm not using it," she replied.

"So, you're going to get another one? How will you use that when you didn't use the first one?"

"Mom, I got a philosophy degree. I work in a pack and ship store. I don't use it because it's not really required to be able to pack someone's documents and send them across the country or to scan office supplies and watch them swipe their credit card."

"What's this new degree going to be in?"

"I'm not necessarily saying I'm going to get another one. I was just making conversation. You asked me what's been on my mind."

"Venice, you're saving up for a store, right? Why spend money on this? Your father and I spent every dime we had on our wedding and honeymoon, and that was a pretty big mistake on our part. If you're just taking a class or two, what's the point?"

"Well, I'd learn something. That's the point."

"To what end, Venice? I took that business course online when I was running the salon. It didn't do anything for me."

"Mom, I'm not you," she replied.

Val was sitting on her sofa, staring at the black screen of the TV in front of her, with her legs tucked underneath her. She had her phone to her ear but was now regretting this call to her mother, which she made weekly, despite the fact that they only lived about thirty minutes apart. She didn't actually remember the last time she'd been over to her parents' house. It was usually depressing there. Her dad

151

would complain about his job. Her mom complained about having to be on her feet all day. They talked about the weather and the dog, and then Val went home.

"No, you're not me," her mother replied. "But you've been saving up for something, Venice. We can't help you financially with this."

"You couldn't with college, either, Mom. And I don't expect you to do anything now. I'm thirty-five years old; soon to be thirty-six. I don't need money from you guys."

"Well, okay. Then, do whatever you want, Venice. If you think taking a class is going to get you this business thing that you don't really need, faster – go for it. I think you have a decent job, and you're making enough money to support yourself. That's really all that matters, isn't it?"

Val hesitated before saying, "Mom, did you ever want something so badly that it ate away at you? Did you ever really dream of something? Think about it all the time?"

Her mom didn't answer right away, but then said, "Not that I can think of. I guess, when I was a little girl, I wanted to be a ballet dancer, but I didn't have the body for it. Why?"

"Because I've never had that, either; that passion for something."

"And this class is something you're passionate about?"

"Not yet, but I want to take something to see if it could be. The ones I looked up so far are in three different areas: one is in business; one is in the arts; the other is a computer course."

"Computers?"

"Yeah, coding basics."

"Coding?"

"Yes, Mom. It's very basic, but I don't know. I think I want to learn new things and see if anything inspires me to pursue something different."

"How much is this going to cost you?"

"Not as much as you'd think. It's a community college, and I'm not enrolling. I'm just taking them individually."

"What does this do to your plan for your store?"

"I don't know yet. I might still do that. It will just take a couple of extra months. I might not do it at all. But this is the first time I've been remotely excited about anything professional in… maybe ever."

"Well, if it's what you want, do it, Venice. But if you're just now starting to focus on your professional life, when exactly will you be focusing on your personal life? I'd like grandbabies, Venice. Your father and I are still waiting; and neither one of us is getting any younger."

"I know." Val chuckled at the change in subject. "And I don't know about *focusing* on it, but I might have an update on that front."

"You have a girlfriend?"

"There's someone special, yes."

"Who is she?"

"It's new, Mom."

"I don't care how new it is. I'm the mother. I get to know when my daughter is seeing someone."

"I haven't talked to her yet about who we're telling."

"Why would that matter? Has she not told her parents?"

"I don't know because we haven't talked about it, Mom."

"Well, just tell me her name, then."

"Jessica."

"Jessica," her mother repeated as if by doing so she'd know just who Val was talking about. "When can we meet her?"

Val chuckled and said, "I literally just said we haven't talked about that yet. It's new, Mom. I don't want to go too fast."

"Then, we can arrange something for a few weeks from now."

"Mom, weeks? How about months?"

"So, you think you'll still be together in a few months? That tells me something."

"I'm glad," Val replied sarcastically. "Look, I'll call you when it's time for that to happen, okay?"

"When? Not if?"

Val hesitated before saying, "I really like her, Mom."

"Is she part of the reason you're making changes to your life plan?"

"She gave me the idea to consider going back to school." Val paused. "And I'm glad for that, because I feel like I've just been walking through life. I don't want that for myself. I want to find the thing I'm supposed to do, the thing that I'm passionate about."

"Well, I'm not sold on the whole going-back-to-school idea; you didn't like it much the first time. But if this Jessica makes you happy and helps me get grandchildren sooner, I guess I can support it."

"Mom!" Val laughed.

***

"I miss you," Jessica said into the phone.

"I miss you," Val replied, holding the phone out so she could see Jessica's face on the screen. "You really had to go back to New York?"

"I did. I'm sorry. I'm contractually obligated to do a shit ton of press for the movie release. That's the actual description in my contract; a shit ton."

That made Val laugh as she tried to focus on Jessica's eyes, and not the lips she wished she could be kissing.

"Is Carol there with you?"

"Glued to my side as always. The girl takes one vacation every million years, so you can expect to see a lot of her."

"You're lying in bed right now. Is she right beside you? Should I be concerned?"

"She's in her own bed, probably arranging my entire life on her calendar app. She has things color-coded. Red means, I cannot miss this thing because it's in a contract.

Yellow means, I can consider missing it if she lets me, but she never lets me. Green means, I can go somewhere if I want, but only if I'm not exhausted from all the reds and yellows."

Val laughed and asked, "What color would a date with me be?"

"You'd get your own color," Jessica replied.

"Yeah?"

"What do you want? I'll tell Carol to add it to her over-organized app."

"I'll take whatever your favorite color is," she replied.

"Green is my favorite color, and it's already taken." Jessica gave her an awkward grin. "I could ask her to alter her system, but you're going to have to make it worth my while."

"Yeah? How do I do that when you're in New York, and I'm in LA?"

"Give me a shot of the girls in that sexy sports bra," Jessica said, wiggling her eyebrows.

"How do you know I'm even wearing a bra?"

"You're not wearing a bra?" Jessica asked and smacked her face with her hand. "I could have been there when you were bra-less? I'm missing out."

Val laughed yet again and said, "How long do you have to be there?"

"Three more long and exhausting days. The studio wants more interviews than I did initially since the movie is looking like a winner. They're trying to double down on the publicity in order to make a run at award season."

"It's already after midnight there, Jess. You should get some sleep," Val told her.

"I don't want to sleep. I miss you."

"I miss you, too," she replied. "And I need to tell you something."

"What?"

"My mom knows I'm seeing someone."

"She does?"

"I told her when I called her about something else," she said.

"Does she know it's me?"

"I told her your name is Jessica, but I didn't tell her anything else."

"You've told me she's okay with you being gay, so I assume she's used to you having girlfriends?"

"Well, she's not used to it because it doesn't happen a lot, but she's fine with it, if that's what you mean." Val paused and then decided to take the risk. "She is asking where her grandbabies are, though. I thought you'd want to know."

"Oh, she's one of those, is she?" Jessica asked with a smile.

"She's wanted grandkids for a while now."

"That would require you wanting those kids. We've talked about that, so I assume you're on board with her having those grandkids?"

"I am."

"Good," Jessica said, nodding. "You can tell her you and I will let her know if and when we decide to take that step together."

"If?" Val asked, staring at the tiny screen, wishing Jessica was lying beside her.

"Am I allowed to say when? I feel like I should say when, but we just started this. We haven't even had sex yet."

"And you're already talking about having my babies?" Val laughed.

"How lesbian of us," Jessica laughed.

"I think, just the right amount of lesbian," Val replied.

"Maddox invited us to a party she's having at the house."

"She did?"

"Yeah, I told her I'd ask you if you want to go. I don't know if things are weird now that you and I are dating, and I've kind of made up with Maddox and Avery."

"You're calling her Maddox now? What happened to

Maddie?"

"Maddie is of the past." Jessica nodded. "I am living in the present and moving into the future with Venice Valentine Russo."

Val smiled and asked, "Do you want to go? It's really up to you. She's your ex."

"I kind of wish we could brush past the awkwardness and get to a point where we're all just friends again without it being between us, but since that's not possible, I do think I'd like to go. I've talked to everyone on my list except for Peyton."

"She's going to be there if she's in town."

"I thought about texting Dani to see if they were, but that's cheating, right?"

"I don't think it's technically cheating, but you're better than that, Morrison." Val winked at her. "You've already conquered Maddox and everyone else. You got this."

"When I come back, can we go out on a date? I mean, a real date, where there's a nice meal at a nice restaurant and some other date-like activity."

"Of course," she said.

"Okay. I'll ask Carol if she wouldn't mind giving a new meaning to the green blocks on my calendar and making the things I can miss blue or something. I don't want any confusion. I'm not missing the green blocks if those blocks involve you," Jessica said.

"Well, I hope she'll consider your request," Val teased.

"I need a lot of green blocks, Venice. I really do miss you. Just falling asleep next to you is my new favorite thing."

"It's mine, too," she replied.

"I should get some sleep," Jessica finally acquiesced as she yawned. "I'll see you in a few days, okay?"

"I'll call you tomorrow night, okay? Even if it's just for five minutes because you're too tired, I want to hear your voice before you go to sleep, okay?"

Jessica smiled and said, "Okay."

CHAPTER 21

"So, you two still haven't…"

"No, I've been out of town in case you didn't notice, Carol," Jessica said.

"She came out of your bedroom in the morning, Jessica. What was I supposed to think?"

"She just slept over. We didn't do anything."

"We got back last night. Why didn't she come over?"

"I was exhausted, and she went out with her friends, Devin and Jana, and a couple of others, I think. They were in Santa Monica. I didn't want to make her drive all the way here. It was late when I got home, anyway."

"Look at you, being so considerate," Carol mocked as she placed a script in front of Jessica's face. "You need to read this one. It's good."

Jessica took it but placed it on the kitchen table and continued to focus on her breakfast.

"I will later, but I need help, Carol."

"Reading?"

"Yes, obviously, I need you to read this script to me because I am incapable," Jessica replied sarcastically.

"Okay. Someone needs to get another few hours of sleep because she's really snappy this morning."

Carol sat down next to her and took a drink of her coffee.

"I need help planning a date."

"A date? You've never asked me for help with dates before. I don't even think you've asked me to make a dinner reservation for you and a date before."

"Well, I'm asking now. You have a boyfriend. He likes you enough to take you to a beach, so that must mean you're at least okay at this relationship thing. I don't exactly have the best track record; and, Carol, I don't want to mess this up. I want Venice."

"In her pants?"

"I want her; all of her. I just can't imagine being with anyone else." Jessica leaned back in her chair.

"Really? It took me a long time to even admit I like my boyfriend, and you're already talking about a forever kind of deal. Are you sure it's not too much too soon, Jess?"

"No." Jessica shook her head. "I'm not, but I was sure with Maddox, and looked where that got me." She shrugged a shoulder. "I know how she makes me feel, and I love that feeling."

"Okay. Well, if you want my help, I'm happy to do whatever. I'm not exactly great at planning dates. I'm usually too busy to go on them because I'm taking care of you."

"I'm surprised anyone would even put up with you, given you're hardly around," Jessica said. "Do the guys you date think I'm a tyrant?"

"Oh, yeah. I tell them all that you're a terrible boss who needs me twenty-four-seven – especially, when I don't feel like putting out – I complain about how much you exhausted me that day and that I just need to sleep."

"You're terrible." Jessica laughed.

"So are you, if you ever talk to the boyfriend," Carol replied, winking at her.

***

"I thought we were going to a restaurant," Venice said.

"We are. Well, we're sort of going to a restaurant," Jessica replied.

They were walking hand in hand from the parking lot down the concrete stairs toward the beach.

"I see no restaurants, Jessica," Venice said.

"What is a restaurant? I mean, philosophically. You have a degree in that, so you tell me."

"What are you talking about?" Venice laughed as they arrived at the sand.

"Kick off those shoes, baby. We're eating dinner on the beach at sunset." Jessica tugged on her hand as she kicked off her own flats.

"We're eating here?"

"There are perks to dating someone with a little money saved to show her girl a good time." Jessica smiled at her and watched as Venice took off her sneakers and held them at her side. "See that?"

"That's a tent."

"Not a tent. It's open in front, facing the water. You're just looking at it from the back. Inside, you will find a waiter who will bring us the delicious food I've ordered ahead of time; and by that, I mean Carol did the actual ordering, but I picked out the food. I've also brought a bikini for me and may have invaded your dresser before we left your place and tucked your one-piece into my bag. A one-piece? Really? You couldn't own a sexier bathing suit, Venice?"

"I do. That one-piece is old. You just didn't look hard enough," Venice said, teasing her. "And what exactly do you expect me to do in a bathing suit, anyway?"

"Conquer your fear, babe." Jessica pulled Venice into her and kissed her.

Several minutes later, they were sitting at a two-person table complete with a white tablecloth and a red-lit candle between them. The waiter had poured them their wine, gave them their appetizers, and then, he'd disappeared. Jessica had paid a little extra for some privacy. The beach was technically a public one, but she had rented it out for the occasion. There were no houses on this side of the PCH in this area, as the cliffs surrounding them were a little too dangerous to build on. A landslide a few years ago had deemed the area unsafe, but there had been three or four of them even before that, so no one wanted to build here. That gave them a little more privacy as the sunset in front of them and the noise of the people several hundred yards away from them, faded and then disappeared with the sun. They ate and talked through their entrées. Jessica told Venice about the other parts of her trip that she hadn't had the time to fill her in on during their daily and nightly calls. Venice kept staring at her in a way that told Jessica she was in this just as deep as she was, and there was something so reassuring about that.

"So, dessert?" Jessica asked.

"I don't know where to fit it. I ate everything on my plate, Jess."

"Then, let's skip it. We can change into our suits, and the caterers can clean up while we swim."

"It's dark, Jess. It's not safe."

"Yes, it is. You'll be fine. It's going to be cold, so we won't last long anyway. I just want to be there with you and hold on to you like I did in the pool. I loved that."

"So did I." Venice smiled at her. "If I do this, you can't let go of my hand, okay? I really hate the ocean."

"I promise. I will not let go of your hand."

Venice looked around and asked, "Wait. Where exactly did you want us to change?"

"Right here, babe."

The space was all of about ten feet by ten feet. There would be no privacy, but there weren't any people around. The caterers were probably back by their van just waiting for Jessica to tell them they could go home. Jessica stood up, reached into her bag, and pulled out a one-piece suit that she tossed to Venice. Then, she pulled out her own black bikini that left little to the imagination.

"Is that a thong, Jessica?" Venice asked when she saw it.

"Yes," she replied, smirked, and turned around to face the side of the tent. "You change first. I won't look, I promise."

"Really?"

"I promise, Venice. Put on the damn suit. The water is only going to get colder from here."

A few minutes later, Venice announced that she had changed. Jessica had used that time to change into her bikini, trusting that Venice wouldn't turn around, either. When they both turned to face each other, Venice's look told Jessica that her choice in swimwear had been a good one.

"I cannot believe you're wearing that, and I'm wearing a ratty old one-piece I bought on sale because I thought I'd join The Y and swim a lot a few years ago."

"I'm enjoying myself just fine; thank you very much." Jessica walked up to her and wrapped her arms around Venice's neck. "I like you in anything, though; even that blue vest you have to wear at work. Sometimes, I picture you only in that blue vest."

"You do?" Venice wrapped her arms around Jessica's back, pressing them together totally. "I like your suit," she said as she lowered her hands to cup Jessica's bare ass.

"It seems like you do." Jessica nodded toward the water. "Come on, babe. You got this."

Jessica pulled her by the hand until they were at the shore.

"This is a bad idea, Jess. There's no one around if something happens."

"There are caterers right back there. I'm sure they'd love to rescue two damsels in distress if something happens."

"I prefer to rescue my own damsel," Venice said.

"For that, you'd have to be out there with me."

"I don't think that's right." The expression on her face told Jessica she was thinking way too much about this.

"Let's go," Jessica said.

"Holy shit! That's cold!"

"Good. You'll be more motivated to get all the way in." Jessica continued to pull on Venice's arm until they were waist-deep in the water. "Okay. Now, we're almost there. A few more steps and we'll be good."

"Feels good now. I don't think we need to go any deeper. I can feel the seaweed. I don't like seaweed, Jess."

"I guess I'm the one rescuing the damsel tonight?" she asked the challenging question, knowing Venice wouldn't be able to resist.

"Shut up."

Venice pulled Jessica into her, instantly wrapping her arms around her waist, allowing Jessica to turn to face her and wrap her own arms around Venice's neck, where they belonged. Her legs moved around Venice's hips and stayed there.

"The ocean's not so scary after all," Jessica said so softly, she worried Venice couldn't even hear it over the sound of the crashing waves.

"Not with you here," Venice replied.

They stayed that way for a few minutes. Venice kissed Jessica's neck, cupped and stroked her ass, and then finally kissed her lips long and slow. Jessica tasted the salt on Venice's skin, and she loved it. She loved this: being held by this woman, holding on to her, and feeling completely and totally wanted for the first time in her entire life.

"We should do this more often," Jessica said.

"We could do part of this more often and leave the ocean out of it," Venice replied.

"You don't want to have ocean sex?" she teased.

"Have you had ocean sex?" Venice asked.

"Do you really want to know?" Jessica asked back, lifting an eyebrow.

"No. Yes. No. I don't know. I mean, I know you're not a virgin. Neither am I. Do I want to know if you've ever had sex in the ocean?" Venice seemed to be asking herself all of the questions, so Jessica just waited. "What about the pool? I assume you've had pool sex. Wait. Do I want to know if you've had pool sex?"

"Venice?"

"Yeah?" Venice finally met her eyes.

"I was kidding. I've never had sex in the ocean." She kissed Venice.

"Pool?"

"Once. It wasn't great." Jessica shook her head. "Thus, I never repeated it. I really am a woman who likes her sex the standard variety." She ran her hands through Venice's hair, allowing Venice's arms to hold her in place. "I prefer a bed." She kissed her lips. "And the lights down low." She ran her hand down Venice's neck to her collarbone. "And maybe some mood music if there's time to turn it on before. If not, I just need the right woman on top of me." Jessica kissed her again. "Inside me." Her hand lowered to Venice's breast, which she cupped. "All over me," she whispered into Venice's ear.

"Jess?"

"Yeah?"

"Can we go home now?"

Jessica whispered, "Yes."

CHAPTER 22

"Hey," Jessica said when Val came out of the shower.

"Hi," Val replied.

Jessica had showered in one of the guest bathrooms when they arrived at her house. She had finished before Val, who showered in Jessica's master bathroom per Jessica's instruction. Jessica was sitting on the side of her king-sized bed, looking up at Val expectantly. Val had thrown on one of Jessica's over-sized T-shirts after the shower and nothing else. Jessica was wearing a shirt as well but had also put on a pair of pink shorts. Her hair was down and a little damp, like she'd tried to blow dry it but didn't finish. Val's was shorter and would only take a few minutes to dry all the way. She ran her hand through it out of habit and heard Jessica gasp.

"I love when you do that," Jessica said.

"Should I do it again?" Val asked.

"Yes," Jessica whispered, and Val was in love with the sound of that word coming out of Jessica's mouth in that hushed tone.

Val ran her hand through her hair again and watched as Jessica clenched the comforter with her fists.

"What else should I do?" Val asked.

"Whatever you want," Jessica said.

Val took a few steps toward her. Then, she knelt in front of her, spreading Jessica's legs apart. Jessica looked down at her, transfixed. Val kissed the inside of Jessica's thigh as she ran her hand through her hair again. Jessica's hand replaced her own and continued to slick back Val's wet hair over and over as Val kissed the softest skin in the world repeatedly.

"In case you ever doubt it, let me make something clear, first, okay?" Val said, running a hand up and down Jessica's other thigh. "I want you." She kissed a little higher up. "I need you." She moved her lips to Jessica's other thigh. "I will call you to say goodnight every night for the rest of my life when we're not falling asleep next to each other if that's what it takes to get you to understand how much I want you." She looked up and into Jessica's eyes as they met her own. "Let me worship you tonight."

Jessica nodded. Then, Val stood up. She reached forward for Jessica's arms and lifted them above the woman's head. She lowered her hands to the hem of the shirt and pulled it up until it was lying on the bed next to Jessica, and her full breasts were revealed to Venice for the first time.

"Is this better than the picture I sent you?" Jessica asked.

"Oh, baby." Val knelt down again and reached for the shorts. "I told you, when I saw you for the first time, it wouldn't be in some picture. It would be because you're here with me, and I'm touching you how I've wanted to touch you since the first moment I laid eyes on you." Val pulled at the shorts until Jessica leaned back on her elbows and lifted her hips. Then, they were off, and Val could see all of her because Jessica hadn't put on any underwear. "Perfect," she whispered.

"Can I see…" Jessica faded out as Val stood and pulled off the only piece of clothing she had on, leaving her naked and standing in front of the most beautiful woman in the world. "Oh, wow," Jessica whispered back.

"I'm no model. I–"

"Stop," Jessica said a little louder. "You're beautiful. You're mine, Venice. You're beautiful, and you're mine, and I want you." She slid back and over until she was lying at the top of the bed. "Make love to me."

Val moved on top of her slowly, wanting to drink her in. Jessica was strong and feminine at the same time. Val slid her hands along her calves, her thighs, and over her taut stomach. Then, she was hovering over Jessica, not touching her anywhere but wanting to touch her everywhere.

"I've never…"

"What?" Jessica asked as she wrapped her arms around Val's neck.

"Felt this way."

"Neither have I," Jessica said, rubbing her nose against Val's.

Val leaned down to kiss her, running her tongue against Jessica's top lip before she sucked it into her mouth. She lowered her body down slowly, allowing each part of her to take in how it felt to be pressed against Jessica bit by bit, sensation by amazingly perfect sensation. When she finally pressed their centers together, she gasped before Jessica could.

"I love you," she said.

She'd said it without thinking, without worrying about whether or not Jessica would say it back. She had said it because she had to say it. She had to tell this woman that she was in love with her, that she wanted everything with her; and those three words, she hoped, would convey that regardless of what Jessica would say next.

"I love you, too," she replied, pulling Val in for another deep kiss.

Val moved her hips into Jessica's, rolling them because she couldn't control herself. Her lips moved to Jessica's neck, which she bathed in kisses between sucking on her pulse point and licking her throat because she just had to taste her. As her mouth lowered, she heard Jessica's soft gasps, and it spurred her on. She finally sucked a hard nipple into her mouth as Jessica's hands played with the back of her neck and hair, tugging on it enough that it hurt, but Val didn't care. She needed more of this woman.

"I want to be everywhere at once," she admitted. "I don't know what to touch next, Jess. I just–"

"Hey, we have time," Jessica said softly, looking down at her as Val kissed her stomach. "We have time, babe. I'm not going anywhere."

Val kissed the same spot again before she made her way back up Jessica's body to kiss her once more. Jessica was right; they did have time. They had all night. They had longer than that. They could have forever if that was what they wanted. Val knew that was what she wanted. Jessica was it. Somehow, a little over a year ago, when Val had been hitting on Avery Simpson, Jessica had been inside that house, possibly making out with Lisa Grandy. That part wasn't what she wanted to focus on, though. Val had spent another year or so after that party not knowing this woman, which seemed so strange to her now because it felt like she had known her forever. She had never felt so desired in her life as Jessica cupped her ass and pressed her down into her body further, requesting more and more from Val's body. She had never felt understood and so supported. God, she had never felt so loved.

Val kissed Jessica's breasts, licking each nipple until it turned back into a hard peak. Then, she sucked on it until Jessica cried out, and Val switched to the other breast to repeat the action. She continued until Jessica begged her to stop because she couldn't take anymore. Only then did Val move lower to her stomach, running her hands up and down Jessica's sides, squeezing her breasts, and kissing the soft skin around her belly button. She moved her lips to Jessica's hip bones, sucking and leaving a mark on each one. Jessica didn't stop her. She just continued to breathe hard as Val lowered still, kissing one thigh and then the other, swirling her tongue against the skin in the same way she was about to swirl it elsewhere.

"I want to taste you," Val said as she hovered her lips over Jessica's center.

"Put your mouth on me, Venice."

"I secretly love that you call me that," Val replied, kissing the woman just above the small amount of hair around her slit.

"Not a secret anymore," Jessica said, running her own hand through Val's hair again. "Never grow your hair out or get it cut any shorter. I always want to do this when you're down there," she added.

Val smiled up at her. Then, she got her first taste. Jessica was wet. She was very, very wet. Val wanted to drink it in; Jessica's desire for her. She wanted to hear the gasps and moans the woman beneath her was letting out, too, but Jessica's legs squeezed her head so hard the moment Val starting sucking on her clit, that Val couldn't hear anything. She swirled her tongue and felt Jessica's hips lift up off the bed, lower back down, and repeat the movement. She then moaned herself when Jessica started pulling at her hair. She squeezed Jessica's breasts and toyed with her nipples until Jessica's hips moved up and down regularly and then faster and faster until her body was twisting, and Val had to press down on her stomach to keep her in place.

"Yes!" Jessica screamed that, and Val could definitely hear it. "Yes! Oh, my God! Don't stop! Don't stop! I'm coming! Yes!"

Val didn't stop until the screaming had ceased, Jessica's hand had loosened, and her hips had stopped. Then, she licked her again, bathing in Jessica's sweetness, and looked up at her.

"Do you want me inside you?"

"Yes," Jessica whispered.

Val moved on top of her, slid her hand between Jessica's legs, and then moved two fingers inside her. She was tight from her previous orgasm, but Val moved slowly enough to give Jessica time to open for her.

"You're mine, Jess." Val kissed her lips, knowing Jessica would taste herself on them.

"Yours," Jessica replied. "Fuck!"

"More?"

"Yes," Jessica said. "Deeper. Fill me up, Venice."

Val thrust a little faster and a lot deeper until Jessica opened for her. Then, she added a third finger, heard the woman cry out for her, and pumped into her fiercely, claiming her beyond the words she'd just said. Jessica was hers. She would always be hers now. Venice knew it in her soul, her bones, and every part of her body that tingled and writhed for this woman.

"I love you," she said again, needing to speak the words over and over now.

"I'm coming!"

Jessica's hips moved in time with Val's thrusts until she was screaming again, coming at Val's touch. Val kissed her, taking her breath and turning it into her own. Jessica's whole body continued to writhe until Val finally slowed and then stopped altogether, lowering herself on top of Jessica. She tried to catch her breath as Jessica did the same. When she tried to pull her hand out, Jessica pressed it back inside.

"Stay?" Val asked.

"Yes. And then, again," Jessica stated. "I need you again."

Val didn't wait. She moved inside her slowly, curling her fingers inside Jessica, searching for the spots that made her whimper, gasp, and moan. When Jessica started to get louder, she moved her fingers out and back in.

"I need you to come for me," Val said.

"Touch me here," Jessica requested, pressing Val's palm to her clit. "And I'll come loud for you."

"Louder than you already have? Venice asked.

"I'll scream your name," Jessica promised as Val lifted up to look down into her eyes. "Venice Valentine."

CHAPTER 23

"GOOD MORNING," Jessica said. "Why didn't I wake up next to you?" She kissed Venice's neck as she wrapped her arms around the woman's waist from behind and pulled Venice back into her.

"Because I was going to make you breakfast and bring it to you." Venice turned her head slightly to kiss her. "You woke up."

"I did, and you weren't there. I'm not a fan of that." She squeezed Venice's hips. "I like it when we fall asleep together and wake up together." Jessica kissed her neck again.

"You've said as much." Venice cracked an egg in the pan. "And I like that, too, but we've got to eat, Jess."

"And sleep probably, too." Jessica was kissing the woman's shoulder now.

"We got none of that last night," Venice replied.

"So… Are you hooking us up with protein so we can go again?" she asked, hoping the answer was yes.

"Maybe," Venice replied.

"Wait. Really?" Jessica turned Venice around in her arms.

"Why is that so surprising?" the woman asked, placing her hands on Jessica's hips after she wrapped Jessica's arms around her own neck.

"It's not. We were just up all night."

"And I want you all day," Venice said, kissing her lips.

"Would you like to start right now?" Jessica asked, lifting an eyebrow. "I would."

"I just put the eggs in the pan."

"I have more eggs," Jessica replied, lowering her hands to Venice's ass and sliding them inside her boy shorts. "I'd like to take these off."

"What about Carol?"

"She does not get to take these off." Jessica lowered herself, sliding Venice's shorts to the floor and kissing the inside of her thighs. "Only I get to take these off you from now on."

"Jess, what if Carol walks in?" Venice asked at the same time she put her hand on the top of Jessica's head.

"She won't." Jessica kissed her again, moving a little closer.

"How do you know?"

Jessica swirled her tongue in the way Venice had done to her many times already but on her thigh, giving her a hint as to what was to come.

"I texted her last night and told her you were staying over. I also may have mentioned that I planned on having hot sex all over this house, and if she didn't want to see anything, she should stay home today." She lightly bit the spot just above the patch of curly hair between Venice's legs, earning a hiss. "She, apparently, does not want to see either of us naked."

"Good," Venice said, pressing Jessica's face into her sex. "Because I want you."

"Happy to oblige, baby," Jessica replied as she smiled.

Jessica loved doing this to Venice. This woman was usually so controlled and didn't seem all that excitable, but as Jessica had discovered many times over the course of last night, Venice could definitely be excitable when Jessica had a hand or her mouth between her legs. She stroked her slowly with her tongue at first and then heard as Venice reached behind her own body to remove the pan or maybe turn off the stove; Jessica wasn't certain which one, but Venice tapped her head, causing her to look up. Then, Venice took two steps to the right. Jessica smirked up at her, moving on her knees until they were away from the stove, and she had Venice against the counter. Then, she started sucking.

"God, that's good," Venice said, rubbing Jessica's head like she was a lamp Venice wanted to coax a genie out of.

Jessica sucked harder and faster before she slid two fingers inside her girlfriend and thrust just as hard and just as fast. Jessica moaned when the rubbing stopped, and the light hair tugging began. It didn't take long. With Venice, it didn't seem to ever take long. Jessica had lost count how many times they'd made one another come the previous night, but she knew Venice hadn't taken more than a few minutes each time Jessica had brought her to orgasm. When she came this time, Jessica looked up at her. Venice's head was back. Her neck was exposed, and Jessica wanted to kiss it, lick it, and suck on it until she made marks all over it.

"I love doing that to you," she said, standing up and moving to Venice's neck to do just that.

As she did, though, Venice turned her around and pressed her to the counter, but she didn't stop there. She turned Jessica around in her arms so that Jessica's back was to her front, and Jessica's front was now pressed to the counter. Then, Venice yanked off Jessica's sleep shorts with ease as Jessica hadn't bothered to put on any underwear. Jessica leaned over the counter, hoping she was guessing right. Then, Venice was inside her with one hand, and the other one was stroking her clit. This wasn't the slow, sensual lovemaking from last night. Venice was fucking her against a counter, and it felt so ridiculously perfect.

"You're so wet, Jess," she said into Jessica's ear.

"I just ate you out in my kitchen. Of course, I'm wet." Her hands had nothing to hold on to, so she pressed her palms against the wall behind the counter. "God, yes! Do whatever you fucking want to me, Venice."

And Venice did. She made her come twice against that counter. Then, the woman turned her around so fast, Jessica had almost gotten dizzy. Venice knelt down in front of her, lifted Jessica's leg over her shoulder, and tasted her, bringing

Jessica to a third orgasm before breakfast. God, there wasn't anything better in life than this.

***

"I can honestly say that I don't think I've ever had so much sex in such a short amount of time," Venice told her a few hours later.

"Yeah? I broke a record?"

"I think you broke all my records," Venice said, running her hands up and down Jessica's sides.

Jessica was straddling her on the sofa at the moment. They were both naked and had remained so since their first encounter in the kitchen. Breakfast had been eggs and coffee along with each other. They'd finished eating and moved to the sofa with the intention of lying around and relaxing, but then Venice had done that damn hair thing, and Jessica had climbed in her lap. Two orgasms later, Venice was running her fingertips over Jessica's bare back and giving her soft kisses on various parts of her body. Yeah, Jessica could get used to this.

"I like breaking your records."

"I like making new ones with you," Venice said.

"Hey, I have a question for you," Jessica replied.

"Okay." Venice looked up at her.

"Let's go out later."

"That's more of a confusing statement than a question; you know that, right?" She laughed a little.

"You know what I mean. That's all that matters. Last night, I wanted to do something special, and I thought the beach was a nice touch for a first date."

"Oh, there were a lot of nice touches last night," Venice said, kissing between her breasts.

Jessica smiled and said, "But we've yet to go out into the real world as a couple. I think we should do it sooner rather than later."

"Why's that?" Venice asked, looking up at her.

"You haven't exactly been exposed to what happens sometimes, when I go out."

"Ah." Venice nodded.

"It didn't use to be a big deal. I was a model. Most people wouldn't necessarily recognize me on the street, but now that I'm acting, and I have a new movie out, it's happening more often."

"Is this a test?" Venice asked.

"Not a test." Jessica cupped her cheeks. "I just think it's important for you to see that part of my life, too. I'm out, Venice. It's no secret that I'm gay. I normally show up stag to events, but that's because I haven't had anyone special for a long time." She paused and smiled widely at her. "Until now. Now, I have you. I'm in love. And I don't want to thrust you into the spotlight if you're not ready, but I kind of want to shout from the rooftops that I'm taken by a woman who looks fucking amazing in and out of a tuxedo."

"You know I have no experience with this, right? I have famous friends, but I'm not famous. I don't know how to deal with cameras and stuff."

"First of all, I'm so glad you didn't just say that you're *kind of* friends with famous people. It shows growth, babe." She winked at Venice. "And second of all, I'll be right there. We don't have to do anything you're not ready for, and if you don't want to go out tonight, we don't have to. It's not a planned thing. We probably won't even be noticed. That would be fine with me. I just don't want to hide you or us from anyone or anything. I love this. I love you."

Venice didn't hesitate before saying, "Then, let's go out tonight."

"Yeah?"

"Yeah."

"Good." Jessica leaned down to kiss her. "Now, let's get in the pool. I owe you swim lessons."

"What?" Venice asked as Jessica climbed off her body.

"Come on."

"We're naked."

"So? No one can see." She moved to the sliding glass door and pulled it open. "If you skinny dip with me and let me teach you how to swim, I'll let you do that thing to me you liked so much last night."

"That's blackmail, Jessica Morrison." Venice stood up and walked toward her all the same.

"Blackmail for a good cause. I don't want to have to worry about you drowning in our pool one day."

"Oh, it's our pool now?" Venice walked through the door out into the backyard.

"It will be someday. I love this house, but if we move in together in the future – which seems likely because I'm kind of obsessed with you – and you don't want to live here, I'm making sure we have a pool, Venice Valentine. A girl needs a pool, especially when she has a hot girlfriend she wants to swim with."

"Fine. You can teach me how to swim, but I get something else out of this deal."

"You want more than just the thing?" Jessica asked, following her outside.

"I want to turn that bad pool sex experience you had into good pool sex with me." Venice stepped into the pool without hesitation.

"Oh, yeah?"

"Yeah. In fact, I think if we start with that, I might be a lot more relaxed when it came time for the lessons."

Jessica smiled as she walked in behind her, feeling the cool water caress her calves, her thighs, and then her still hot and sensitive center.

"Well, then; where do you want me?"

Venice moved quickly until she had Jessica pressed to the infinity wall; her legs spread as wide as they would go. She slid her hand between them, and Jessica's head went back as she stared up at the Los Angeles sky as the woman of her dreams made her come again and again, completely changing her view on pool sex forever.

CHAPTER 24

"So, dinner in a restaurant or dinner on the beach?" Jessica asked her as they shared a dessert.

"Well, I guess that would depend on the restaurant, but I'll take dinner with you anywhere," Val replied, winking at her.

"Nice one," Jessica teased. Then, Jessica's eyes moved behind Val. "And we almost made it."

"What?"

"Don't turn around. It'll only give them a shot. There are paps out there."

"Paparazzi?" Val asked.

"I thought we'd make it. We've paid the check and everything." She placed her fork on the near-empty plate between them. "So close."

"What do you want to do?" Val asked.

"Nothing different than what we were going to do; leave when we're done with dessert and go home."

"Your place or mine?"

"Yours is technically closer."

"You're sleeping over, right?" Val asked.

"I hope so," Jessica replied, smiling at her.

"Are you sure you want–"

"Have you found a new roommate yet?" Jessica cut her off.

"I have a few leads," Val replied. "Honestly, I haven't put that much effort into the search. I've been a little busy lately."

Jessica's smile widened, and she said, "How long can you go without one?"

"Not long. Well, I guess that depends. Technically, I have money saved up. I could use it if I need to, but it's saved for the store."

"Have you landed on that yet?"

"Buying a franchise?" she took a drink of the coffee Jessica had ordered for her.

"Yeah, I haven't asked. Are you still thinking about doing that?"

"I don't know." Val shrugged a shoulder. Then, she tugged at the skinny tie to loosen the knot at her neck. "You were right, I think. I've never really figured out what I want to do. I kind of just latched on to the idea of owning my own store because it seemed like the logical next step, and I could at least say that I had my own business."

"But?"

"But I don't know that that's what I want. Is it crazy to still be trying to figure this out at my age?"

"No." Jessica shook her head. "I was a model for a long time before I realized I wanted to act."

"That's different, though." Val leaned forward. "Don't take this the wrong way, but models kind of have a shelf life, right? You were always going to have to find another career."

"That's true and not true at the same time." Jessica matched Val's posture. "I was a very successful model, Venice. I have enough money to make it through with my investments for the rest of my life, probably. If I wanted to, I could retire on some island and never work again. And even if I still had to work to be able to support myself, I didn't know that I wanted to act. Some models do it, but I didn't expect it to be me. Commercials are one thing, but TV shows and movies are a whole other thing."

"What changed your mind?"

"I think it was Lennox and Kenzie, honestly." Jessica looked behind Val again through the window that led to the street. "I thought what they did was cool. I wondered if I could do it myself and decided to audition for something, thinking I had nothing to lose. I didn't get it, and I didn't get the next one, either. But, by then, I already had the bug. I got the third one, though, which was a bit part, and now, I'm a lead in a feature film, and there are photographers outside the restaurant where I'm eating with my girlfriend." Jessica placed her hand palm up on the table. "And don't think I didn't notice that shirt and tie combo. You look sexy as hell, babe." She winked at her.

Val smiled at her, rolled her eyes, and said, "To answer your earlier question, I could probably go the remainder of my lease without a roommate. It will just put a dent in my savings. It doesn't matter too much. As of right now, it's going to take two years, at minimum, and more likely, three or four years before I can get the place because I have no collateral; so what's a few extra months?"

"How long is your lease?"

"Another seven months," Val replied.

"I'm going to ask another question."

"You have a skill with these questions that sound like statements, Jess," she teased.

"Do you want money to–"

"Jess, I don't want your money." Val placed her hand into Jessica's open palm on the table. "That's not what this is about."

"I know that. Venice, I know that. Just let me finish, okay?"

"Okay," she replied hesitantly.

"If you want to open this store, I will loan you the money."

"I can get a loan from the bank. I just have to get some collateral first," Val explained.

"Venice, I can co-sign for you. I've done it for a couple friends before with their businesses. If you don't want that, I can arrange for the loan to be through me. You can pay me back if it's important to you, but I could also just give you the money, babe. Please don't make it a pride thing, okay? What I'm asking you is this: if you could have the start-up money part of this equation solved, whether it be by the bank or by me, what would you do right now?"

Val thought about it as Jessica's fingertips lightly grazed the soft skin of her palm.

"I wouldn't take it," she said and realized at the same time.

"Why not?"

"Because I don't want to own a pack and ship franchise."

"What do you want, beautiful?" Jessica asked.

"To figure that part out. I guess I want to find my own dream."

"That's amazing, babe." Jessica squeezed Val's hand. "And I'm here for whatever that is, as long as I can be with you."

"I think I'm going to take a couple of classes this summer at the community college."

"Yeah?" Jessica's eyebrows lifted. "Can I help you study? There can be prizes if you do well."

"What kind of prizes?"

"I was thinking they would involve nudity," Jessica replied.

"Those are prizes I can get behind."

"Or in front of or inside or beneath or–"

"Jess," she whispered and laughed at the same time.

"Hey, don't re-sign your lease when the time comes, okay?"

"That's months away. I'm not even thinking about that yet."

"I was just thinking that I don't want you to sign for another year after that; even six months."

"My apartment's that bad?"

"You are so dense sometimes," Jessica said, chuckling and leaning back. "Babe, I'm saying that I'm assuming we're still going to be together in seven months; that I'm going to be even more in love with you than I already am, and that I'd like us to consider taking the next step at that point."

"Next step? You're talking about moving in together?"

"In seven months," Jessica replied. "Not tomorrow. If it's not right, then, it's not right." The woman looked out the window again. "I might not be ready; or you might not be. If that's the case, we'll talk about it, but – I don't know – this feels right to me. You feel so right, and I don't think I'd want to keep waiting if we can move toward something together."

Val smiled at her gorgeous girlfriend and said, "Okay. We'll see how it goes, but I'm good with that."

"Yeah?"

"Yeah."

"Okay. So, tell me about these classes." Jessica leaned in closer. "What are you taking?"

"Nothing major."

There was a loud sound that came from their right. Val turned to see a photographer standing in the lobby of the restaurant, taking pictures of Jessica, and probably her, too, and the manager of the restaurant was trying to push the guy back outside.

"Shit," Jessica said. "We should go before there are more of them out there. I swear, it's not like this all the time. It's just because the movie is doing well, and also probably because I'm a woman dating a woman."

"Hey," Val said.

"You ready?" Jessica moved to stand.

"Jess, it doesn't bother me."

"Really? It's annoying to me."

"Let's get out of here, okay? But you don't have to rush me through the crowd because you're afraid I can't handle it. I don't care. I'm not exactly a fan of being on some gossip site later, but if it means I get to be with you, I'm fine with it; especially, because these intrusive cameras mean my girl is kind of a big deal."

"Not exactly." Jessica laughed and stood. "But let's go to your place. I'd like to try to get at least a few hours of sleep tonight, but that will be after."

"After what?" Val asked as she stood up.

"After I pull that skinny tie off and slowly unbutton that shirt." She winked.

They made their way toward the front door of the restaurant just as the photographer was shoved through the door and onto the sidewalk. Jessica thanked the manager. Val opened the door for her girlfriend and was met with flashing bright lights and a lot of noise. She'd been prepared for the cameras, but not for the yells coming from the people – mostly men – holding the said cameras.

"Jessica, who's your date?"

"Jessica, what's her name?"

"Are you together?"

Jessica took Val's hand and walked through the door with her.

"We're just heading to the car, guys," Jessica said. Then, she reached inside her purse and passed Val her car keys. "Can you drive?"

"Sure," Val said, taking them.

"Guys, we don't want to run over any feet," Jessica said, distracting them as she let go of Val's hand when they arrived at the car. "Have a good night." She waved at the cameras.

Val climbed into the driver's seat. Moments later, Jessica got in beside her.

"That's intense," Val said as she started the car.

"Too intense?" Jessica asked, turning her face toward Val and away from the cameras outside the car.

"No, I'm good. Plus, I get to drive your fancy car."

"Well, I figured my soft butch would like to drive her femme home," she teased.

"You're never letting that go, are you?" Val laughed as she pulled out of the lot.

CHAPTER 25

"WHY do you look so nervous right now?" Venice asked as they walked up to the front door.

"Because I'm about to see Peyton for the first time in a while, and she probably knows what I'm going to try to talk to her about," Jessica replied, taking a deep breath.

"You don't think she'll listen?" Venice asked.

"I don't know. I can only hope Dani warmed her up a little for me, or that Maddox inviting us to this party means something to her. I know that I hurt all my friends, but Maddox was the one I hurt the most. If she forgives me, shouldn't Peyton?"

"I guess we'll find out." Venice squeezed her hand and rang the bell. "If she doesn't today, she will in the future. I don't know Peyton as well as the rest of you, but from what I do know, she's a good person. She's just very, very loyal, so when someone–"

"Hey, guys," Avery said as she pulled open her front door. "Come on in."

"Thanks," Jessica said, putting on her fake smile.

It wasn't fake because of Avery. She liked Avery a lot. The woman had not only made things easier on Jessica when she had gone to her office, but she had welcomed Jessica into her life with Maddox knowing about their history. Not all women would be kind enough or secure enough in their relationship to allow their girlfriend's on-again, off-again ex-girlfriend into the home they shared. The smile was fake because Jessica was very nervous and anxious. A hand squeeze from Venice, though, was enough to make her feel a bit better. When that hand moved to the small of her back as they walked through the door, it gave her the confidence she needed to not only talk to Peyton but to seek her out first and see what happened.

"Everyone is in the living room for the most part," Avery began. "There are a few in the kitchen and a couple outside." She pointed through the sliding glass door where Jessica could see Maddox pushing little Sienna on the baby swing and Dani standing in front of them, taking either a video or a series of pictures with her phone.

"We brought wine." Venice held up the two bottles they'd chosen together. "One red. One white."

"You didn't have to do that, but thank you," Avery said. "I'll put them in the kitchen. Help yourself to whatever you want. I think this is about it on the people. We only invited a handful."

"Are we celebrating something?" Venice asked. "Jess only told me we'd been invited to a party."

"I guess, technically, Maddox wanted to celebrate my business expansion. With the funding we've secured, we're in a really good place right now. She likes to celebrate that stuff." Avery shrugged slightly. "It's also kind of a mini send-off for her, though. She's going to Brazil, Peru, and Colombia with a documentary film crew studying the effects of deforestation on the Amazon and the surrounding areas. She'll be gone for a few weeks."

"I didn't know that," Jessica replied. "But, I guess I have been out of the Maddox loop for a while."

"The opportunity just came up. She's taking all the stills and working alongside the crew. She's very excited. I, however, am very nervous."

"You're not going with her?" Jessica asked, wrapping her arm around Venice's side and pulling her into her.

"No. I can't leave right now even if I wanted to, but I'm also not a big fan of hiking through jungles. Maddox loves that adventure stuff. I am much better suited to an office and a computer." She smiled. "I'm so happy for her, though. She had to get all the vaccinations, and I'd hate that, but she smiled all the way through because she was going to get to do this amazing thing."

"Does it bother you that she's going alone?" Venice asked Avery. "I know it would bother me if Jess was going somewhere like that without me."

Jessica smiled as she looked over at her girlfriend and gave her a kiss on the cheek.

"The crew will be with her. I trust them to keep her safe. I'm sure we'll both slow down one day, and then we'll get to spend more time together. I will miss her, though, but that's Maddox, isn't it? I love her like crazy for who she is, and she loves me for who I am. It means that sometimes, she goes off on these trips, and we have calls and FaceTime, and it also means that I get some alone time to continue to work on the app and my other hobbies."

"Which are?" Jessica asked.

"Recently, I've been getting into decorating this house." Avery looked around. "Maddox can be a little distracting at times." She glanced out the window at her girlfriend, who was laughing with Dani and Sienna. "She also does not care what color I paint the walls. So, when she gets back, she'll be surprised." Avery smiled when she looked back at them. "I love that woman." Her smile widened.

Venice looked over at Jessica and mouthed the words, 'I love you' to her. Jessica kissed her lips in response, hoping that would convey that she felt the exact same way.

"So, who else is here?" Jessica asked.

"Lennox and Kenzie are putting Liam down for a nap in our room. Peyton is in the living room, talking to my brother and his boyfriends, Dario and Magnus."

"Boyfriends?" Jessica checked.

"You heard me right," Avery said. "They're all together. It confuses the heck out of me, but it seems to work for them."

"Well, okay," Venice said.

"I'm going to find Peyton. Is that okay?" Jessica asked her girlfriend.

"Of course. I'll grab you a drink and wait for you."

Jessica kissed Venice once more before she walked into the living room to find Peyton holding on to her son, Jordan, and three men sitting around talking and laughing about something. She waited until there was a lull in the conversation. Peyton turned to look at her and gave her an unreadable expression.

"Can we talk?" Jessica asked, thinking she'd get right to the point.

"Okay," Peyton replied, standing up. "I'll be back. You three, behave." She winked at them and shifted Jordan in her arms. "Maddox and Avery's room?"

"Kenzie and Lennox are in there," she said.

"I know. They're putting Liam down. I'll relieve them and put Jordan down with him. They're used to napping together," Peyton replied, walking past Jessica and not really waiting for an answer.

They arrived at the closed door, and Peyton opened it with her free hand, being careful not to make too much noise.

"Hey, he's almost out," Lennox told her.

Kenzie was lying on one side of Liam, and Lennox was on the other. It was such a perfect picture, Jessica's heart hurt a little. She wanted that. She wanted the wife and the kids, and all the diapers, screaming, and baby puke that came with moments like this; the quiet ones, where you could spend together as a family. Lennox was running her fingers through Kenzie's hair. Kenzie was rubbing little Liam's back. They looked at each other and shared an intimate smile. Then, they looked at Peyton and Jessica, who had entered the room with a clearly exhausted Jordan.

"Do you want us to put him down, too?" Kenzie whispered.

"Jess and I will put him down next to Liam," Peyton said. "You guys go, enjoy the party. We'll be quiet when we talk about that thing Jessica's been avoiding talking to me about."

"Okay," Lennox replied, sliding out of bed. "Let's go get something to drink, Kenz."

Kenzie slid out with her. Lennox waited by the door to take Kenzie's hand, and they walked through the door. Peyton moved to the bed and the pillow barriers Kenzie and Lennox had placed. She moved one a little farther out and bounced Jordan a few times on her hip until his eyes were closed. Then, Peyton placed him next to Liam, who wasn't much younger than her son was. She rubbed both his back and Liam's at the same time. Jessica just stood there and watched; again, feeling that tinge of pain, wanting these special moments for herself and for the person she would share her life with.

"So, are you going to start, or am I supposed to?" Peyton said in just above a whisper.

"Are you sure it's okay in here?" She pointed to the sleeping babies.

"Yeah, they're out. Sienna was such a pain in the ass when she was this age. She was a great baby, but when it came to naps, she'd always fight back. Jordan usually just crashes, and Liam's pretty much the same way."

"You spend a lot of time babysitting?"

"I don't really consider it babysitting. Lennox is like my sister, and Kenzie is like my sister-in-law. That makes this little guy my nephew. All of our kids will grow up as cousins."

"That's pretty great." Jessica smiled.

"We're waiting to see what Maddox and Avery will do. If they get going on that soon enough, we'll add more to our growing brood."

"Growing?" Jessica asked.

"Dani and I aren't done." Peyton shrugged a shoulder at her. "We want at least one more; maybe two."

"That's great, Peyton."

"What about you?"

"Me?"

"You and Venice? You two are together."

"Yeah, but we're not thinking about kids just yet." She chuckled a little under her breath. "We're still thinking about where to have our next date more than making wedding plans and going to see the doctor about putting a baby in me."

"But it's serious between the two of you?"

"I love her," Jessica replied and sat down in the armchair next to the bed.

"She's my friend," Peyton said, looking at her.

"I was, too, once," Jessica replied.

"And that didn't exactly end well."

"It doesn't have to end at all, Peyton," Jessica said, leaning forward in the chair. "I made a terrible mistake. I think about it every single day. I think about the look on Maddox's face when I disappointed her over and over. I'll never get that out of my mind; and I used to think I didn't deserve to."

"Used to think?"

"Venice got me to realize that I did make a mistake, but I'm not a bad person. I'm not going to excuse how I behaved or that, back then, I blamed Maddox for all of it instead of taking responsibility for my own actions. All I can do is apologize for what happened and be better. I want to look forward, not back anymore. I want to own what I did and never do it again because I can't stand to hurt anyone like that."

"So, you're promising me you won't hurt Val?" Peyton asked, running her fingers through her son's baby fine hair.

"I can't do that. I'm sure I will. I'll do something that hurts her, but it will be unintentional, and I will do anything and everything I have to in order to make it up to her. I can see forever with her, Peyton."

"You could see forever with Maddox."

"And I was wrong." Jessica smiled at her. "Maddox was my first real love. I thought that was it because it was the best it had ever been for me. But when I look back now, I can see that Maddox and I were never meant to be. The way it ended was terrible, but it would have ended, Peyton. Maddox and I would have been miserable if we were still together now. I look at Avery and how she just told me Maddox is going away for several weeks, and she's good with that. I think back to how I handled it when we had to spend time apart, and I hated it. I wanted her around all the time. I didn't understand how she could just be okay for weeks at a time without me. I thought that meant she didn't love me, but Avery just gets it." She paused and watched Peyton smile softly at her son. "Venice and I seem to get each other in that way. I need someone that wants me; needs me. I always have. Venice wants to be needed; needs to be needed. It just works with us."

"Then, I'm happy for both of you."

"But, I don't know what that does with us, Peyton." She pointed between the two of them. "You know I've been making the rounds, trying to apologize to everyone."

"Dani told me. Then, Len told me. Finally, Maddox told me. I can see I'm last." The woman lifted a perfectly sculpted eyebrow at her.

"For good reason." Jessica lifted her own eyebrow back.

"Maddox is one of my closest friends."

"I know, and–"

"Just let me finish, okay?" Peyton said softly.

"Right. Sorry." She leaned back in her chair.

"But you were, too, Jess," Peyton continued. "It wasn't just about what you did to Maddox. That was bad, but you ruined our group when you did it. It was the six of us back then. It didn't last long, but it was you and Maddox, Dani and I, and Lennox and Kenzie. You know how important family is to me, and you were part of my family."

"I know," she said solemnly.

"You messed that up."

"I know."

"But I'm not above forgiveness," Peyton said. "And you hurt Maddox more than you hurt me. She invited you here today, so I think that says something." Peyton paused as she looked down at Jordan and Liam. "If you want to be part of this family again, Jess, I don't have a problem with it."

"Really?" she asked, leaning forward again.

"When I look at him, I think of the future and the life I want him to have. I think of Sienna, too, and the ones we might still have. I look at little Liam and think about how amazing it is that Kenzie and Lennox decided to have kids after all. I want all of them to grow up surrounded by love. I don't want Sienna and Jordan to hear about how their mom couldn't forgive a friend. I want them to know that forgiveness is a part of life; no one is perfect. And if you own up to your actions and ask for forgiveness, someone will find a way to give it to you."

Jessica let out a deep breath and said, "Thank you."

"You don't have to thank me, Jess. Let's just try to move on now, okay? If you and Val are on that path together, your kids would be my nieces and nephews, too. That's how this works. Just be good to each other, okay?"

"We will," Jessica said and with a smile.

"Let's leave these two to sleep," Peyton told her, standing up and taking the baby monitor off the table. "I'd like to see what my wife and daughter are up to. My guess is, they're out there just laughing about something. They do that together a lot." The woman smiled widely. "Dani is always smiling. I think Sienna got that from her."

"What about Jordan?" Jessica asked as she stood.

"I think he takes more after me. He seems contemplative." Peyton glanced down at him, tucking the pillow in more securely. "It's either that, or he just has to poop a lot."

CHAPTER 26

"Hey, how did it go?" Val asked when Jessica joined her out in the backyard with the rest of the party.

"I'll tell you all the details later, but it went pretty well." Jessica smiled and took her hand.

"That's so good, babe," Val said.

The backyard hadn't been decorated for a party. It wasn't really much of a party now that Val thought about it. It was more just a gathering of friends. There was no music playing over speakers or any decorations put up. It was just eleven adults and three kids hanging out at Maddox and Avery's place. Val looked around and saw the most famous women in the world, realizing she was standing amongst them, and feeling like she actually belonged for the first time.

"Thank you," Jessica whispered into her ear before she turned Val to face her. "I don't know that I would have done all of this without you."

"What are you talking about? Of course, you would."

Jessica's arms went around her neck. Val pulled her in, loving the pastel orange sundress her girlfriend had worn for the occasion.

"Maybe, but I think it would have taken a lot longer."

"Well, you got me to do some things, too, so maybe we're even," Val said, pressing their foreheads together.

"Calm down, lovebirds. There's a child present," Dani said, pretending to cover little Sienna's eyes.

"We're not making out in front of her," Jessica replied, kissing Val and pulling away a bit.

"You can make out in front of her if you want,"

191

Peyton said as she moved toward Dani. "She's walked in on Dani and I making out in the living room at least three times." Then, she kissed her wife. "Hey, babe. I put Jordan down for a nap with Liam."

"This one might be right behind them." Dani placed her hand on the top of Sienna's head."

"No nap," Sienna said.

"Told you." Peyton looked over at Jessica.

"Is everyone outside?" Maddox asked as the only three men present made their way out to the yard.

"Yeah. You told us to come out here," Tony, Avery's brother, said.

"Right," Maddox replied.

"She looks nervous," Jessica whispered to Val and moved in front of her so that Val could hold on to her from behind. "I know why," she added, still in a whisper.

"Why?" Val whispered back, kissing Jessica's bare shoulder next to the strap of the dress she planned on taking off later.

"Just wait," Jessica said.

"So, I invited you all over for a few reasons," Maddox began. "First, Avery's business." She looked at her girlfriend, who was only standing a few feet away. "My girl is crazy successful." Maddox laughed a little. "Dr. Simpson has gotten herself a major investor and will be expanding her app empire soon."

There were cheers from the crowd.

"That's my little sister," Tony mock-shouted and earned some laughs.

"Second, and it's not really a celebration thing, but I'm heading to South America for a few weeks, so this is my informal send-off until I come back with some kick-ass pictures and amazing stories to share with everyone." She took a few steps toward Avery. "And I'm going to miss this one here like crazy." She took Avery's hands in her own. "Because I don't just want her to be my girl anymore; I want her to be my wife." Maddox let go of one of Avery's hands and reached into her pocket. "Avery Simpson, will you marry me?" She held out a ring that Val couldn't see much of from where she was standing.

"What?" Avery asked, covering her mouth as her eyes got big. "I didn't know you were doing this."

"That's how a surprise works, Avery," Maddox replied. "Will you?"

"Oh, yes," Avery said, apparently realizing she hadn't actually said that yet.

Everyone applauded and cheered as Maddox slid the engagement ring onto Avery's finger and pulled her in for a long kiss and a hug after. Val pulled Jessica back into her and kissed her neck again.

"I love you," she said.

"I love you, too," Jessica replied.

"You okay with this?"

"Maddox getting married to the love of her life?"

"Yeah," Val replied.

"Absolutely." Jessica turned around in Val's arms and added, "I plan on doing the same thing with mine."

Then, she kissed Val.

***

"Jess, I'm heading out," Val said.

"Your class doesn't start for over an hour."

"I know, but it's the first one. I don't want to be late," Val replied.

They had spent the night at her place after spending several nights in a row at Jessica's place. Val had run out of clean clothes, and despite the fact that Carol had offered to do her laundry, Val had asked Jessica if she'd stay at her apartment so that she could leave for her first college class in over a decade from her own place. They hadn't spent a night apart since their first night together, and Val wouldn't have it any other way. She knew when Jessica picked her next movie, she would have to travel for it and for the press

193

part, too, but she'd be okay with that because it was what Jessica wanted. They had already talked plans for how they could see each other during long trips for work and made rules that they would call each other at least twice a day, if not more. Maybe for some couples, that was a lot. For Val and Jessica, though, it was what they both wanted.

"You're so cute," Jessica said, wrapping her arms around her neck. "Look at you in your button-up shirt and your backpack."

"You're mocking me, aren't you?" she asked.

They were standing in Val's bedroom. She'd woken early, nervous about her first day. Jessica had been asleep up until right when Val opened the door, trying to sneak out to avoid waking her sleeping girlfriend.

"I am not. I'm actually very turned on right now," the woman replied.

"Jess…" she said, taking Jessica's hips and pulling her into her body. "We can't. I have to go."

"You have tons of time."

"I'm already dressed," Val argued.

"I can help with that," Jessica said with a smirk.

Jessica unbuttoned her shirt one button at a time. When she got to the bottom one, she opened the shirt, revealing Val's sports bra. Val dropped the backpack to the floor.

"You're killing me."

Val reached for Jessica's T-shirt and lifted it over her head.

"I can see you putting up a big fight right now," Jessica teased as she unbuttoned and unzipped Val's jeans. "You clearly don't want to have sex right now," she said sarcastically.

Val shoved her back onto the bed, reached for Jessica's panties, and pulled them off, all while Jessica laughed at her. She then kicked off her own jeans and underwear and removed her bra before she knelt in front of the bed and yanked her girlfriend toward her.

"I can't focus in my first class if I'm thinking about doing this with you."

"Aren't you always thinking about doing this with me?" Jessica asked, placing her hand on the top of Val's head, encouraging it closer to her sex.

"Yes," she said.

Then, she licked her.

"You could teach a class on this," Jessica said.

"On licking your pussy?" Val asked, licking her again and looking into Jessica's now dark eyes.

"Yes," she replied in a hushed tone.

"First, I like to lick you up and down. I love tasting you all over my tongue." Val flattened her tongue and pressed it against Jessica's sex.

"Fuck, babe!"

"Next – and this is really important…" She licked her slowly. "– is varying the speed. Your pussy seems to like when I go fast and then slow and then fast again. Is that right?"

"Yes!"

Val played with her girlfriend, licking her top to bottom and bottom to top, going fast and then slow.

"After that, there's the swirling."

"Shit," Jessica let out just as Val swirled her tongue around her hard clit. "Yes."

She moved her tongue in small, focused circles, feeling Jessica's hips move and her hand tighten in her hair.

"But, sometimes, you come faster than I want, so I have to slow down."

"What? No," Jessica said, staring down at her.

The circles became more unfocused before she lowered her tongue to Jessica's entrance and slid it inside.

"The big finish," she said.

Then, she slid two fingers inside Jessica, without waiting a moment longer, and moved her tongue back to her clit.

"Yes!"

Val licked and sucked as she thrust inside her. It didn't take long before Jessica's hips were thrashing, and Val had to use her free hand to hold her down. When Jessica came, Val wondered if her neighbors would hear her, but she didn't care. She was making love to the woman of her dreams, and now, her reality.

"That was amazing," Jessica said.

"It was." Val rested her head against Jessica's thigh. "Hey, you know that thing we talked about doing when we were at your place, but you didn't have one?"

"Yes," Jessica said, running her hand through Val's hair and giving her an expression that told her she'd be more than up for what Val was talking about.

"Well, we're at my place now, and I do have one."

"And you want to fuck me with it?"

Val stood up. Jessica slid back on her bed until her head was resting against the pillow. Val climbed on top of her, placing a thigh between Jessica's legs.

"In every room, and on every surface of this place." She kissed her hard.

"Where is it?" Jessica asked when she pulled back for air.

"In my drawer."

"Get it, baby. I want you to use it."

"I will." Val rolled off of her and onto her back. "But later tonight. I have a class to get to."

"What?" Jessica asked, sitting upright.

"I will be back after work. I will do anything you want then." She stood up.

"But you got naked. I was going to–"

"I'm going to sit in class all hard and ready for you, Jess." She looked down at her sexy girlfriend. "When I come home, you can do whatever you want to me. Then, I'll strap on and–"

"Take me against every surface?"

"And in every room," Val added, leaning down to kiss her again.

"Hey, I love you." Jessica wrapped an arm around Val's neck and pulled her back in for another, quicker kiss.

"I love you, too," she replied, smiling at Jessica.

"I'm so excited for you, taking these classes. I hope you find whatever it is you're looking for, babe."

"Well, I've had some good luck recently in that department already." Val winked at her.

Jessica kissed her stomach and the space between her breasts.

"Did you make a decision on that other thing we talked about after Maddox's party?"

Val stood still, running her hands through Jessica's long hair as she stared across the room at the new photo Jessica had had framed and then hung on the wall of Val's bedroom. It was of the two of them taken by Maddox that day after she'd proposed to Avery. It wasn't taken with one of her professional cameras but was a candid Maddox had taken with her phone. Val was standing behind Jessica, kissing her shoulder, which was one of her favorite things to do. She could just make out her smile during that shoulder kiss and could easily see Jessica's happy expression.

"It's crazy, Jess," she said.

"Is it?" Jessica kissed her in the same spot again. "We love each other."

"What if something goes wrong?"

"That's why it's such a good idea," Jessica replied, looking up at her. "I know we talked about you moving in when your lease is up, but we spend every single night together, Val. The college is closer to my place. It's not all that far from the store. Plus, I want you around all the time."

"I know. I want that, too."

"And Carol is already used to you being there. That's a big deal. She's never gotten used to anyone before."

"I'll take that as a compliment," Val said, smiling down at her.

"If you move in sooner, we can have a trial period. If we can't stand to live together, you'll still have this place. If you move in after your lease is up, and you can't stand living with me, you'll have to find another place." Jessica paused, and her expression shifted.

"What's wrong? Where did you go?" Val asked.

"I don't want anything to go wrong, Venice." Her hands moved up to Val's shoulders and then ran down over her breasts to rest on her stomach.

"Neither do I." Val covered Jessica's hands with her own. "Let's do it."

Jessica's smile was perfect.

"Really?"

"I'm basically living with you already, and if I am, there's not much here I need to move over to your place." She leaned down to kiss her. "Let's go all-in. Let's be crazy."

Jessica fell back onto the bed, bringing Val with her.

"There's no one I'd rather be crazy with than you," Jessica replied.

Val kissed her for a long time, not caring about how, just minutes before, she had wanted to get to class early. When she left the apartment, she drove to campus and parked her car. Then, she made her way to her classroom, which was empty. She immediately hopped on the Wi-Fi and went to the website to order the flowers. This time, she chose red roses, knowing exactly what they meant. She pressed the order button, choosing to have them delivered to her store. When she got to work later, she'd route the email over to her girlfriend, and Jessica would undoubtedly come to pick them up. Then, they'd go back to Val's place, set the flowers up, share a meal, and make love all over her apartment. Tomorrow, they'd wake up and start planning Val's move into Jessica's place. She smiled as the professor walked into the room along with a few other students, who had, apparently, had the same idea about being early. She was about to embark on two journeys at the same time. One, she was only beginning. The other? Well, she was already in love and planning her life with the woman she now knew would one day be her wife.

EPILOGUE

V AL was pressed back against the rocks. Jessica was on her knees in front of her, lowering her pants to the sand and gravel mix beneath them. Val wasn't one for public sex, but from what she could tell, no one could see them, and her girlfriend was already on her knees, kissing her stomach and tugging at her boxer-briefs. She wasn't exactly planning on telling Jessica to stop now.

"You're already wet," Jessica said as she ran one finger through Val's wetness.

"I've been waiting all day for this," Val replied.

"Are you sure you don't want to wait a little longer? You're all about anticipation. I could pull your pants back up and make you wait."

"No," Val told her. "Please."

Jessica smirked up at her, slid two fingers inside her, and placed her mouth over Val's sex. It was true; Val had been waiting all day for this. That morning, they had made love in their bed, which, even after many months, was still something she couldn't quite believe. She'd touched Jessica for hours, making her come over and over again, and they had shared a light lunch out in the backyard after. Jessica had then also given her another, now pretty unnecessary swimming lesson in the heated infinity pool. Val had learned enough of the basics to never have to worry about her swimming ability again. After that, they'd gotten ready for the party. Jessica had been trying to get her hands all over Val all day, but Val had wanted to wait until later. She loved the feeling of being turned on. She loved forcing herself to wait like this and then letting Jessica do whatever she wanted to her. Every time, it made the orgasm so intense, she thought about waiting longer the next time. Then, Jessica would do something that drove her so crazy, she couldn't wait anymore.

Tonight, Jessica had worn a gorgeous red and black strapless dress with three-inch red heels. That had been enough to make Val want her again, but they'd left for the party instead, not wanting to be late. She had driven them in Jessica's car. Jessica had placed her hand strategically on Val's thigh, running it up and down slowly and then moving her fingers over Val's center a few times, making Val even crazier. As much as it was pure torture to her, it was also perfection. She wouldn't have it any other way.

They'd greeted their friends when they'd arrived. They'd even taken a few photos and had a drink. They had sat on the sofa by the fire. Val's arm had been around Jessica, and Jessica had burrowed into her side. Val could feel her warmth. She could also feel the woman's heartbeat, which was much faster than normal, meaning Jessica was anticipating something, too. When Jessica said she was cold due to the back door being opened and closed repeatedly as people went outside and came back in, Dani was kind enough to find them a blanket. Val draped it over Jessica mostly, but also over her own lap to make sure they would both stay warm. Then, Jessica's hand then snaked up under her tuxedo shirt, and her fingertips grazed Val's skin before her nails raked across it, causing Val to growl inside. When Jessica's hand lowered and ended up cupping Val over her pants, Val knew they needed to either take care of this fast or not touch each other until they got home.

She'd stood, pulling Jessica with her. Her girlfriend was not helping. She laughed as they went outside; Val claiming she needed some fresh air. That was when Jessica mentioned the rocks she'd heard so much about; the ones that many a couple had gotten busy behind and that could only be seen from Dani and Peyton's balcony. By the time they got there, and Val looked up, Dani and Peyton were nowhere to be found, so when Jessica got down on her knees, Val could not wait for her to make her come.

"Yes," she gasped out as Jessica moved inside her and against her.

"Worth the wait?" Jessica asked.

"Babe, don't stop. My clit is throbbing. I need to come."

"Tell me," Jessica said, kissing the spot beneath her belly button.

"Fuck me," Val replied instantly.

"And?"

"Suck me."

"My pleasure," Jessica said, lowering her mouth again to take Val's clit between her lips.

It didn't take long. Val came when Jessica found that spot she always seemed to find. Val looked down at her girlfriend and knew she would propose to her one day. She'd known that for a while, but it often hit her in moments like this that Jessica was her other half. They fit. She somehow fit with a supermodel-turned-amazing-actress. They had a home together now. They were thinking about getting a dog and planning the next part of their life together. Val hadn't ever found someone she wanted those things with. She smiled down at Jessica, who was pulling Val's underwear and pants back up for her.

"I love you," she told her as Jessica stood up.

"You better. I just went down on you in this dress," Jessica said, kissing her deeply and pressing her a little farther into the rocks.

"Can I?" Val asked, sliding a hand under that dress and landing on the inside of Jessica's thigh.

"You didn't get enough this morning?" Jessica asked, kissing her neck.

"I'll never get enough," Val replied.

She slid her hand into Jessica's panties and found her wet. Jessica pressed into her as Val stroked her clit softly and slowly.

"You're going to tease me?"

"No, I'm going to make you come," Val replied,

stroking just a little bit faster and harder.

Jessica kissed her and pressed her palm flat against the rock behind Val to help hold herself up. Val wouldn't let her fall, though. She'd hold on to her forever. When Jessica came, Val stole the moan in a kiss. When she came down, Val moved her lips to Jessica's nose and forehead. She listened as Jessica tried to catch her breath, not hearing the waves of the oceans crashing not that far away, but only hearing Jessica's breaths in her ear.

"I love you so much," Jessica said.

"Then, let's go celebrate the new year together with our friends. It's our first one as a couple. I want my midnight kiss," Val said, smiling at her.

"You get all my midnight kisses, Venice Valentine," Jessica replied.

***

"So, how was the sex?" Peyton asked.

"What?" Venice said.

"Please, we all came out to the beach, and you two were missing. There's only one place you could go," Peyton replied.

"Babe, leave them alone." Dani slapped Peyton's arms playfully.

"It was amazing, to answer your question," Jessica told her, winking at Peyton as she sat down on one of the blankets laying on the sand about twenty feet from the water. "What this one can do with her–"

"Jess!" Val blushed instantly and was hoping the darkness outside would block her embarrassment from view.

She sat down next to her girlfriend, who was still laughing at her. Lennox and Kenzie were sitting on the other side of Maddox and Avery and were next to Peyton and Dani. It was close to midnight now. There was something in the air that made the world feel exciting and new, even though time was relative in Jessica's opinion. She undid the top button of Venice's tuxedo shirt. The woman always looked sexy to her, but in that untucked shirt, with a bow tie undone around her collar and a pair of tuxedo pants with a pair of black and white Converse and that amazing hair, Venice looked perfect. It was like she was built for Jessica. Hell, maybe she was. It certainly felt that way at times. It definitely felt that way in the bedroom, but also even in how they were with each other.

Venice loved holding her. Jessica loved being held. Venice loved texting her throughout the day just to check to see how it was going, and Jessica loved being thought of like that. Venice loved that she always replied. Even if she was busy, Jessica always replied. Venice was a pretty clean and organized person, and so was Jessica. Venice didn't need a lot of fancy stuff. And even though Jessica did, Venice never gave her a hard time for it. Jessica didn't try to buy Venice the fancy shoes she'd buy for herself. She just picked out those Converse for her and watched as her girlfriend's eyes went wide with happiness over the simplest of gestures. Jessica waited because she knew Venice would slide in behind her, wrap her arms around her, and kiss her shoulder. Venice always did that, and it made Jessica feel safe. It made her feel loved, like she wasn't alone anymore.

"So, third year in a row," Lennox said.

"We're getting too old for this," Maddox replied.

"It's our first time," Venice said.

"Are you sure you want to do this? I think they're all crazy," Jessica said.

"Let's be crazy," Venice whispered their motto into her ear.

"So, have you picked the dresses yet?" Kenzie asked.

"I have mine. Maddox still isn't sure if she wants a dress or a suit," Avery replied.

"I'm leaning toward suit."

"You'd look great in an all-white suit," Peyton said.

"I can see it," Dani replied.

"We're thinking something casual. We don't want a whole big thing," Maddox said. "Just something small."

"I'm your maid of honor. I don't think I've ever done anything small," Dani said.

"That's mainly me, babe," Peyton said. "You are fully capable of giving Maddox a small, casual wedding. If I were the maid of honor, there would be four hundred guests, a few elephants, a couple of tigers who'd carry the rings, and probably fireworks," the woman added.

"That's true," Lennox said, laughing at her best friend.

"I chose wisely, then," Maddox said.

"Well, I'll also probably be the size of a balloon by the time you two walk down the aisle, so it's better that I'm not in the wedding party."

Peyton and Dani had tried for kid number three. This time, Peyton would carry their baby. She'd gotten the news that they were pregnant in early October, so she was now four months along.

"You cannot deliver in the middle of our wedding, Peyton. Maybe we should move it. We haven't sent the save-the-dates yet, and we're not going overboard, so we could postpone until June or July," Maddox suggested.

"You guys are not planning your wedding around us," Peyton said, resting her head on Dani's shoulder and placing a hand on her stomach.

"It honestly wouldn't be a big deal," Avery said. "Maddox and I want to be married, but we don't care as much as most people about the wedding day. It's mainly for our friends and family."

"Well, July would be good for us," Lennox said. "Kenz is filming in Toronto all May and June, so we were going to have to fly in for the weekend, but she'll be done by July."

"What about you two?" Maddox asked, looking at Jessica.

Jessica smiled at her and said, "We'll be there whenever it is, Maddox."

"July?" Maddox asked her fiancée.

"July is good with me," Avery said. "And we'll have another little one there to celebrate with us." She pointed at Peyton.

"You guys can't wait, like, a full year before popping out a kid, can you?" Lennox asked, laughing at Dani and Peyton.

"We've always wanted a big family," Dani said, placing a hand on top of Peyton's. "Peyton has been looking for the right time to carry our baby, and she's taking this whole year off to write and work on the new album. The timing was just right. Plus, Sienna and Jordan are both good babies."

"I'm happy for you guys," Venice said. "And Jess and I are happy to babysit."

"Hold on… You're offering babysitting services?" Lennox asked. "Kenz and I could use a night off."

"It's not babysitting when it's your family," Peyton said, looking over at Jessica.

Jessica nodded and said, "And we're happy to watch any of the kids. It'll be good practice for us." She leaned back against Venice's front. "Right, babe?"

"Right," Venice said.

"So, are we going to find out now, or are you waiting until after the new year?" Lennox asked.

"I don't know that I want to stand out here and celebrate after we're all soaked," Kenzie said.

"We should do it now," Dani said.

Peyton straightened up and asked, "I'm sure you all remember our first two gender reveals?"

"How could we forget? You took swings at a piñata for a good five minutes until you finally actually hit the thing, and pink candy came out," Lennox said.

"For Jordan, there were all blue fireworks," Maddox added.

"Peyton planned both of those. I planned this one," Dani said. "Simple. Our best friends, sitting on the beach with us right before the new year, and just us telling you with no frills and no fireworks."

"Those will probably come at the baby shower, right, Lennox?"

"How many baby showers do I have to plan for you two? You have literally everything," Lennox argued but laughed at the same time.

"I can plan it," Kenzie said.

"You want to plan Peyton and Dani's baby shower?" Lennox asked her wife.

"I've never done it before. You did all the work. I'd like to try," she offered.

"Done," Lennox said, kissing Kenzie's cheek.

"A minute until midnight," Avery said, looking over at Maddox.

Maddox looked back at her and smiled, kissing her lips briefly. Jessica turned her head slightly back to Venice.

"I'm so happy," she said.

"Me too," Venice replied.

"Okay. Are you guys ready?" Peyton asked.

"Let's do it," Maddox said, standing up.

Avery joined her. Kenzie and Lennox stood as well. Dani helped Peyton stand. Jessica and Venice stood up, too, but held onto each other, not having experienced this yet.

"Thirty seconds," Lennox said.

"Are we really going to do this every year?" Kenzie asked.

"Twenty seconds."

"If we do, eventually, we'll need walkers to get out into the water," Dani said.

"Ten seconds."

"Guys?" Peyton asked.

"Yeah?" a few of them said at the same time.

"We're having twins," she said.

"What?!" all of them, except for Dani, said at the same time.

"Happy New Year!" Avery shouted.

All eight of them rushed into the ocean. Jessica hadn't been expecting it would be this cold, but *freezing* would be how she'd describe it. She instantly found her girlfriend, wrapped her arms and legs around Venice, and pulled her in for a kiss.

As strange and crazy as this might seem to others, for some reason, this was a tradition started that night Maddox had met Avery; the same night Venice and Jessica had been at that party and missed each other.

It was probably a good thing they had, though. Jessica hadn't been ready for Venice then. Maybe Venice would have been ready for her, but Jessica was still just so disappointed with herself and her actions, that she hadn't even moved into accepting the fact that she owned them. Venice had helped her move forward in her life.

"Happy New Year, babe," Venice said.

"Where'd your bow tie go?" Jessica asked.

"I don't know. It's probably in the ocean now," Venice said, laughing at her.

"Damn. It completed the look." Jessica ran her hands through Venice's hair. "I'll buy you a new one. You can wear it for me some other time."

"Oh, yeah?"

"Yeah," Jessica said, kissing her again.

"Can I at least get a Happy New Year first?"

"Happy New Year, my love," Jessica said softly against Venice's lips.

***

"Hey, it's five in the morning. What are you doing out here?" Jessica asked, rubbing Val's shoulders from behind the sofa.

"I'm studying."

"You're between semesters. What are you studying?" Jessica asked, leaning over and kissing her neck.

"It's the book for next semester. I'm trying to get a head start."

"You're really excited about this, aren't you?" Jessica

207

asked, moving around the sofa to sit down next to her.

"I am," Val replied. "But it's early, babe. I'm sorry. I didn't mean to wake you."

"Did you even go to sleep? We didn't get back from the party until after one," Jessica said.

"No. I tried to fall asleep, but after you were out, I came here to try to get started on some stuff for a couple of my classes."

"Because that couldn't wait until January second?" Jessica teased.

"I'm excited about something for the first time in my life. Well, I'm always excited about you, but I mean, with other stuff."

"Nice save." Jessica placed her head on Val's shoulder. "Tell me about it."

"Go back to sleep, babe." She kissed Jessica's head. "I'll tell you about it later."

"No, I want to know," Jessica said, moving her legs underneath her. "Come on. Tell me."

"Well, I'm taking two business classes and three computer classes. It's the most I've taken so far, so I think I'm a little nervous, but Avery gave me a couple of online courses she thought were pretty good, dealing with the kind of programming I'll be learning. I was going to start one of them."

"You really like this stuff, huh?"

"I do. Avery and I have been talking about it since we met, but – I don't know – recently, as her company's gotten bigger, I've gotten really interested in what they do there."

"An app to help people sleep better?"

"The stuff that they do to make that. I think I like it. I know I liked the two classes I took last semester."

"I love seeing you like this," Jessica said, running her hands through Val's hair, which was one of Val's favorite things in the world. "So excited."

"It's the first time it's happened," Val said, turning to her. "Thank you."

"For what?"

"Jess, for everything." She cupped Jessica's face in her hands. "Babe, you've literally paid for my tuition."

"So? That's part of this. What's mine is yours, Venice."

"You've tolerated me working full-time and going to school, too," she said.

"Because I know this is what you want. Besides, you always make time for me." Jessica kissed her.

"And now, you're making it possible for me to quit the store and just focus on school so that I can get a degree faster. You knew how hard it was for me to balance everything last semester, and you're making it possible for me to go for this, to really go for it."

"I will do anything I can to help you do whatever you want to do. You don't have to thank me. I love you. I want everything you want for yourself for you."

"Thank you anyway," Venice said.

"You're welcome, I guess." Jessica winked at her. "How about I make us some coffee?"

"Jess, go back to sleep. I can do this later if you want to go to sleep together."

"I always want us to go to sleep together, but you're into this. I want you to do it. I'll make some coffee, and you can study. We can take a nap later today."

Jessica kissed her on the cheek, stood up, and made her way to the kitchen. Val smiled as she turned back to her laptop and textbook on the coffee table. Jessica had worn her down after her summer session at the community college. Val hadn't wanted her to pay for things just because she had the money to do so, but Jessica had pointed out that they were in this together in all ways now. She'd convinced Val to apply for a state school and go for a program. Val had gotten in but hadn't yet declared a major. Jessica helped with the tuition for her fall semester, but now that Val was pretty sure her course of study was going to be difficult, she wasn't sure how she'd be able to manage the store, go to all her classes, study, and be a good girlfriend and a friend who was somewhat involved in planning a wedding for Maddox and Avery.

Jessica had suggested that Val quit, which hadn't gone over well. That had mainly been due to Val's pride. She'd always had a job. She had worked for everything. Nothing had ever just been handed to her. But after a long talk with her mom, who loved Jessica from their first meeting, Val realized she was being ridiculous. After accepting Jessica's offer, she'd put in her notice. They'd celebrated their first Christmas and New Year together, and now Jessica was waking up early with her, bringing her coffee, and encouraging her to study for a class that hadn't even started yet.

"Okay. Coffee, just the way you like it," Jessica said, sitting down next to her again. "Now, where do we start, or am I just in your way?"

Val turned to look back at her like she was nuts and said, "You could never be in my way, Jess. You are my way."

Jessica gave her a soft smile that disappeared as she lifted her coffee to her lips. Val could also make out a light blush on her girlfriend's cheeks, which she thought was adorable. She picked up her own coffee, blew on it for a minute, and took a long drink, letting it slightly burn her tongue because she hadn't slept and needed the caffeine. Then, she opened the course she'd just paid for based on Avery's suggestion, and made the video full-screen, pulling back at her laptop in order to let Jessica see, too. She then reached for her notebook and placed it in her lap, feeling a little silly since she was a thirty-six-year-old freshman, but accepting it anyway because it felt so good to finally be interested in something.

"Okay. Are you ready? It's about an hour long and is all about app coding basics. Avery suggested I start there and build my own test app for some practice."

"What's it going to be?"

"I have no idea," Val said but turned to her and added, "But it's so cool, isn't it?"

"Did you just say something was so cool?" Jessica laughed at her. "You're very cute."

"I'm going to press play now, so if you want to get some sleep, now would be the time to go to bed."

"I'm sure I'll fall asleep just by watching this. I'm not nearly as interested in it as you are, remember?"

"If you do, you can fall asleep on my shoulder. I like you there."

"That is so nice of you," Jessica said, resting her head back on Val's shoulder and looking toward the laptop.

"Okay. Are you ready?" Val asked again, reaching for the trackpad to press play.

"Let's be crazy," Jessica replied.

Made in United States
Orlando, FL
18 November 2021

10508543R00132